the
law of
loving
others

the
law of
loving
others

kate axelrod

razOr
bill

An Imprint of Penguin Group (USA)

A division of Penguin Young Readers Group
Published by Penguin Random House
345 Hudson Street
New York, New York 10014

USA / Canada / UK / Ireland / Australia / New Zealand
India / South Africa / China
Penguin.com
A Penguin Random House Company

ISBN: 9781595147899

Printed in the United States of America

1 3 5 7 9 10 8 6 4 2

For Judy and Leon Thurm, always.

chapter

1

IT was a Friday in the middle of December, the day after Daniel and I had finished our finals, and we were leaving Pennsylvania for New York. The sky was heavy and gray as we left campus and drove toward town, which was mostly quiet. At the second traffic light, I jumped out and ran into a coffee shop on the corner. I grabbed two hot coffees and a chocolate croissant stuffed into a waxy paper bag for us to share. It had snowed earlier in the week and the bare branches were still covered in a sheath of ice. Winter in Pennsylvania was bleak, but still there was something beautiful in its nearly silent emptiness. We drove south toward the interstate, past miles of fields punctuated with farm houses, small squares of red in the distance—an easy calm before the suburban rush of Walmarts and Olive Gardens and vast parking lot after parking lot.

We'd only driven a handful of miles when I turned toward Daniel and kissed his shoulder.

"Daniel? I think I have to pee. I'm sorry. I know we just left, but I do . . ."

"Okay, it's fine. We have like a quarter of a tank left anyway. We'll stop when it runs out. Like an hour and a half?"

"Are you kidding?" I asked. "I can't tell if you're kidding or not."

"I'm kidding," he said and he smiled, displaying a bottom row of crowded teeth. Daniel had told me recently—after I'd commented on how endearing I'd found them, a rare imperfection in his otherwise flawless face—that he'd somehow persuaded his parents and orthodontist to remove his braces several months early, because he refused to start ninth grade with all that clunky metal attached to his teeth. I'd loved hearing this about him, and how assertive he had been even then, at fourteen, when I'd been at the peak of my own insecurity.

"You weren't kidding! You're such an asshole."

Daniel slid his right hand between my legs. "It's so cold," he said. "Warm me up. And yes, of course I'm kidding, but if you want"—he gestured backward with a twist of his neck—"there's an empty Snapple bottle back there. You want?"

"Okay sure, no problem." I reached behind the front seat and leaned over to grab the Snapple bottle. I unbuttoned my jeans and began to unzip my fly but then stopped, smiled at him.

"I dare you," Daniel said.

"Well, if you dare me . . ."

"Double dare you," he said.

"*Double Dare*! Remember that show?"

"Of course. I used to watch those reruns all the time. When I was little, all I wanted to do was get covered in those buckets of green slime."

"If we get married, can we try to go on *Family Double Dare* together?"

"Yes!" Daniel said. "They'll have to bring it back on the air. That can be our honeymoon, straight to Universal Studios. So romantic."

We had been dating for about four months—the entire first semester of my junior year, which, in the strange, warped way that time moved in boarding school, felt significant. We'd sat next to each other the first day of our American history class, and then exchanged a flurry of e-mails before hanging out one night after school, in the beginning of September. Daniel had somehow managed to procure a bottle of whiskey, and we sat on a patch of grass behind my dorm, took long sips from the stout, amber bottle. We played this game called "Eye-rhymes" where you have to think of two words that were spelled the same but sounded different. *Daughter* and *laughter*. *Rough* and *dough*. *Good* and *food*. We alternated back and forth until Daniel was tipsy and I was drunk and could no longer think of appropriate pairs, and then I began demanding all sorts of word play from him.

"Anagrams, go!"

"Oh, I know this one. How about wolf and fowl?"

"Way to go!" I said. Then, "Homophones!"

"Pear and pair," Daniel offered.

"Great!"

"Fair and fare."

"Look at you!" I said.

"Mail and male."

"You. Are. Amazing. Can I tell you a story?"

"Please," Daniel said.

I sat up and rearranged myself so that I was sitting cross-legged, facing him. "When I was in second grade, we were having a homonym lesson, homophones, whatever they're called. And the teacher kept asking us to give examples. And I shot my hand up, so excited, and said 'version and virgin.' I mean, *what* was I talking about? I was seven!"

"What a racy second-grader."

"I know. I really was."

I took a slow sip of whiskey, and when I was done, we made eye contact for a brief moment before he kissed me. It was only an instant, but still I was struck with that dizzying feeling: something is happening. Something important is happening to me *right now*.

❋

DANIEL was a junior also, but he'd been at Oak Hill Friends since ninth grade, and I had transferred as a sophomore. He was from Manhattan and had a certain laid-back way about him—he was confident and self-possessed and made me feel at ease, too. Transferring in as a sophomore had been a difficult thing—the rush and eagerness of freshman year had subsided, and students no longer roamed around in packs trying to stave off loneliness, or the fear of upperclassmen. I had gone back and forth about going away to school, conflicted because this wasn't the sort of thing anyone in my family had ever done (we were a family of worriers, overprotective, anxious, and on a more superficial level, we weren't the sort who carried the monogrammed tote bags or wore the Patagonia fleeces that screamed prep school). But I'd also been nurturing a fixation on boarding school since the beginning of seventh grade, when I spent one rainy October afternoon watching a marathon on TBS that included *Dead Poets Society* and *School Ties*. Even as Brendan Fraser's Jewish character was cruelly snubbed by his blue-blood classmates, I felt myself longing for that sort of prep school life. It was then that I began to romanticize the idea of boarding school: the old dining halls ornamented with delicate chandeliers and bronze plaques, the libraries with arched ceilings, long cherry-wood tables, and stained glass windows. It was all so sophisticated in a way that I was not. I even idealized the loneliness—imagined myself staying in on a Friday night, immersed in some nineteenth-century British novel or writing away about a depressed confessional poet.

Once ninth grade began (and all its complicated politics), anything was more appealing than the boredom I felt at my suburban high school—a boredom that seemed to be the worst kind of ordinary despondency. I was tired of being held hostage to the younger version of myself, who had never gotten below an A on an exam, had never clashed with anybody. And so it wasn't until then that I felt more ready, *less hesitant*, to even apply.

But still, by the beginning of eleventh grade, I wasn't entirely happy at Oak Hill, hadn't fallen into a group of friends in a way that felt organic and right, and meeting Daniel had added a sort of welcome levity to my life at school. It was as if suddenly my life *was* there. My mind was no longer elsewhere, counting the days until I could go back to Westchester and see my friends from home, waiting eagerly for small holiday weekends and other excuses to leave campus.

Of course there were still times when I had my doubts about Daniel; it wasn't as though things were perfect between us. As I'd told my friend Annie on the phone, he wasn't a reader—and that was a potential issue—and sometimes he'd cancel plans with me so he and his friends could get fucked up and do crazy stuff like light old furniture on fire, and why was he so obsessed with ice luges? But I liked how unpretentious he was, so uninterested in posturing about writers or philosophers, especially compared to other people at Oak Hill. Once I'd walked into the locker room after swim class and two girls, while peeling off their navy Speedos, were arguing about who was the hottest of some eighteenth-century philosophers (I only dimly recognized their names, but I remember that David Hume was the pronounced winner). Daniel didn't take himself too seriously, and mostly he just made me laugh. He was a wonderful companion and my chest ached when I left him after lunch to go to class. *Heartburn!* I would say, and this became our thing, always giving each other little packets of Tums as parting gifts. *Heartburn!*

✳

WE drove east on I-80, hitting pockets of traffic, people slowing down when the roads were windy and sharply curved, especially cautious of the snow packed into the mountains to the east. In the fall, driving home for Thanksgiving had been a beautiful trip; the foliage along the interstate was so bright—deep orange-and-red leaves ornamenting the otherwise dull and unchanging stretches of highway. But that day, in the middle of December, everything cloaked in white, the trees and brush blurred into a single graying landscape.

By the time we hit the New Jersey border, both of us were restless and bored. We'd been playing "Fuck, Marry, Kill" for twenty exits, and had used up everyone we knew from school, everyone we'd already made out with, plus some obvious celebrities.

"Okay, we need to get a little more creative," I said. "Burger King, McDonald's, Wendy's."

"Should proximity to the highway have any bearing on my decision?"

"Nope, just go."

"Okay, then I guess I'd kill Wendy's, fuck McDonald's, and marry Burger King," Daniel said.

"Really? Fascinating. Okay, *New York Times*, *New Yorker*, *New York* magazine."

"Oh god, that's hard. Okay, I guess I'd fuck *New York* mag, kill the *New Yorker*, and marry the *New York Times*."

"What! That makes no sense. Obviously you should kill *New York*

magazine, fuck the *New Yorker,* and marry the *New York Times.*"
That I even knew the distinction between these magazines was
something novel—the Oak Hill library received the *New Yorker* each
week, and though I hadn't ever read it at home, it was something I
looked forward to at school, a way to keep up with my peers who
always seemed to know a little bit more than I did about esoteric
writers and high-brow intellectuals.

"Sorry, Em, no can do."

"Of course you'd fuck *New York* magazine."

"I almost don't want to even ask you what that means," Daniel
said.

"You'd sleep with anyone with a glossy cover."

"That makes no sense," he said, "and actually, I have a weird feeling you're getting jealous about this."

"Not *this,*" I said. (I was jealous, always. I tried to control it but
every time he looked at his texts and I saw his inbox filled with messages from Lily, Jen, or Vicky, I'd feel my stomach tense up, filled
with the fear, the anticipation, of infidelity.)

"I'm sorry that you think I've slept with everyone in the world,
but you just have to get over it. It's not like you were a virgin when
we met."

"I basically was."

"That's not a thing . . . You either were or you weren't. And you
weren't! You lost your virginity when you were fifteen too."

"Yeah, but that was with my *boyfriend.* I've never had like, 'casual'
sex." The very nature and meaning of that phrase was not something

I really understood or felt connected to. I wondered if there would be a time when such an expression would just roll off my tongue, when I would be able to say honestly, in an offhand way, *oh yeah I slept with that guy one time, it was nothing.*

"Okay, I'm not indulging you anymore. Enough! You want me to kick you out onto the highway?" Daniel said.

"Okay, I'm sorry!" I unbuckled my seatbelt for a moment, leaned over to kiss his neck, the side of his face.

"All right, let's get back to the wholesome stuff. Here are your choices, regular bacon, turkey bacon, soy bacon."

❄

WE made a list of the things we wanted to do in the month we'd be home: spend a weekend or two at Daniel's parents' house in the Berkshires, try to see some smaller movies that never made it to our small town, maybe go to a Kurt Vile show at Bowery Ballroom. Daniel's parents owned an apartment on Central Park West—and I grew up in a suburb about twenty miles north of the city. We figured we'd see each other a couple of times a week, and would probably spend most weekends together.

By four thirty, the sun was already starting to set. We were somewhere in Rockland County and the sky was huge all around us—bands of purple and pink were setting behind the jagged mountains.

"I think I already miss this," I said. "Post road-trip blues."

"I know, baby. You're nostalgic for everything, all the time."

"Am I?"

"Always," Daniel said.

I called my mother, who'd wanted to know if I would be home by dinner.

"I should be back pretty soon," I told her. "Daniel's dropping me off within the hour, I think."

"Okay, sure."

"Everything okay?" I asked.

"Yup, uh-huh." I heard some shuffling in the background, but mostly it was the absent quality in my mother's voice that made me wonder.

"What are you doing?" I asked. "You sound distracted."

"Sorry, I'm just in the closet going through my clothes. I was planning to go through some old dresses and skirts that I never wear anymore and get a big donation over to the Salvation Army. But there's something—I don't know, something strange happening."

"What do you mean?"

"These dresses aren't mine," my mother said.

"Are they mine?" I asked her. "I don't think I have stuff in your closet but maybe I do?"

"No, no, it's not like that. I'll tell you when you get home."

"Okay, I'll see you in a few hours. Love you," I told her.

"Love you too, sweetie. Drive safe."

chapter
2

WHEN I arrived home, my family and I had something akin to traditional Shabbat dinner. This was something we rarely did; we were culturally Jewish, not at all religious, and that night it looked as though we were a family who savored these customs, lighting a pair of slim ivory candles and blessing the challah. But more likely it was just that there was a special on roasted chicken at the supermarket, and my mother thought it would be a nice thing to do.

She had always been the sort of mother who was extremely attentive, attuned to my moods and needs. When I was a child, I'd come home from school and just by my posture, she could tell if I'd had a bad day, gotten into a fight with one of my friends, or done badly on a math test. She was a micromanager, too—if I was hungry, she would peel and section clementines for me, toast and butter bagels, even when I was well into my teens. But that first night back, something was off; she was inattentive, preoccupied. I wondered if maybe this was just what started to happen when you got older—and in going away to boarding school, wasn't I expected to tend to myself, as I'd been doing for months already? And that seemed normal; I was seventeen—I didn't need to be babied. But it also felt abrupt, because during all my other visits home, we had quickly fallen back into old routines; I would sleep late and my mother would come in around noon to wake me, ask me if I wanted breakfast. Did we want to drive to the mall to do some back-to-school shopping?

"Emma," my father said at dinner, slicing asparagus up into tiny pieces with the side of his fork, "did Mom tell you we're thinking of redoing the basement?" He was tall and thin and balding, with a thick, graying beard.

"She didn't."

"At least part of it. I've been toying with the idea of turning the bathroom down there into a darkroom. What do you think?"

"Sounds cool. Are you still teaching photography at school?"

"I'm not right now, but planning to in the spring. I'll probably teach an elective just for juniors and seniors." My father had been a history teacher at the same public school in Westchester for almost twenty years; this was also the school that I'd recently transferred out of (and his being there was not totally unrelated to why I'd left). He taught a number of different classes, though what he really loved was the comparative American-studies elective. He was beloved at the school, and yet constantly battling the administration on what he could teach and how. The central problem always came down to this: he never understood how he could possibly teach an *apolitical* history class. The simple retelling of history *was* of course a political act! It always troubled him when people didn't understand (and this was something he had ingrained in me as a young child) how the stories put forth by textbooks year after year were the rich white man's story, not the stories of the enslaved and underprivileged.

My father, I could tell, was simultaneously envious and proud of the fact that I was at Oak Hill. A private school—and a Quaker one nonetheless—granted a freedom that he was unaccustomed to. It was unabashedly progressive, offered no AP courses so that teachers wouldn't have to "teach to the test," was the first boarding school in the country to accept people of color, and had a course catalog as thick as any small liberal arts college. (And ultimately they had offered me the most generous financial aid package, so that was why I had accepted.)

My mother was sitting at the head of the table, her back to the refrigerator, which was crowded with magnets displaying cat jokes and photographs of various children in our extended family. She was picking some dark-meat chicken off a thigh, examining it closely, and then she looked up.

"Oh stop," she said, her voice was quiet but oddly cheerful. "It's really not their fault."

"Huh? Not *whose* fault?" I asked.

"What?"

"You just said, 'It's not their fault.'"

"Oh nothing, sorry." She looked down again and scooped up a forkful of rice.

My father brushed her wrist. "You okay, sweetheart?"

"Yeah, I'm fine, sorry. Just a long day, four lessons this morning, back-to-back."

"Your mom is becoming the talk of the town around here. Some crazy mother from Scarsdale called and asked if she could give a piano lesson to her two-year-old."

"No way. The kid is actually two?" I said.

"Something like that."

"Are you gonna do it?" I asked her.

My mother was quiet for a moment, and my father immediately interjected.

"She'll have to see if the scheduling will work out—the kid has SAT tutoring after day care, so it might not work."

"Good one, Dad."

I watched as my father slid some of his chicken onto my mother's plate, pushed it toward her with his knife. She was the kind of woman who people were always trying to feed. She had a small waist, dainty wrists, slim fingers, and even my seventy-eight-year-old grandmother was always encouraging her to eat more. Before she moved to Florida, my grandmother often came by with potato salads or bagels and lox, brownies wrapped in tinfoil.

"Thanks, honey," my mother said, "but I'm okay, I promise. I ate a big lunch." Then she looked at me, asked if we'd hit any traffic on the way back from school.

"Here and there. It wasn't terrible."

My father asked if Daniel was a good driver. "I never trust those city kids," he said.

"He actually is! His dad taught him to drive stick shift upstate when he was fifteen. He's barely a city kid."

"Oh right. The second home, of course."

"Speaking of second homes, I'm gonna go over to Annie's after dinner."

"Well, of course," my father said, "you've been home for forty minutes and it's already time for you to leave."

"Very funny. Annie was away over Thanksgiving so I haven't seen her in so long."

"Emma," my mother said, and turned to me. "Before you leave, can you just take a look at the closet with me? It won't take long, I promise."

"Yeah, sure."

"I'll clear the table," my father said. "You guys can go."

❅

MY mother and I went into the master bedroom, which suddenly struck me as so old-fashioned and outdated. Something about the way the sun had drained the color from the wallpaper, and the clutter of photographs, the framed artwork from when I was a child. The walk-in closet was narrow but long, with a single lightbulb dangling from the ceiling. There was a shoe rack on the floor that held a dozen pairs of pumps and leather flats, shoes that my mother had bought decades ago and probably hadn't worn since the eighties.

"Okay, look," she said. Her small, unadorned hands brushed past various fabrics—cotton skirts, velvet and silk dresses. "Just look."

"I'm looking. And I don't get it," I told her. "All your stuff is here."

"I know it seems that way, but just look closely."

"I don't understand what you're talking about, Mom. All your stuff is here. This is the same stuff that's been in your closet since forever. Maybe that's the problem. You've had all of it for so long, you don't even remember it."

I realized that I sounded exactly like my mother and I felt a faint prickle at the back of my neck, a warning that, unaccountably, there'd been some strange shift in her thinking. Maybe she'd just had a long day or a bad night's sleep, but I felt a sliver of panic creeping in.

"No, Emma, just listen to me. I know everything looks the same, but it's not. Everything's nearly identical, but that's the problem. Someone switched it all, as if I wouldn't notice. Look at this dress." She lifted up the hem of a floral dress. "These flowers used to be tulips and now they're lilies."

"*Someone switched them?* What are you talking about! You're being crazy."

Was she drunk? Was this a brain tumor? Or was she just getting older—would this be the place where that irrevocable shift toward dementia would start to occur? But my mother was barely fifty. It seemed absurd, way too early.

"*I'm crazy?* What about the person who broke into the house and stole my clothing and then tried to replace it?"

"Mom, you're being ridiculous and you're actually freaking me the fuck out. Please just stop!"

I'd only cursed at my mother one other time that I could remember. I was in the sixth grade and we'd gotten into this huge fight over practicing the violin, which I hated and was terrible at. I could never quite get my fingers coordinated enough, was never able to play without thinking, couldn't just feel the music and move effortlessly, the way my mother seemed to be able to do with every instrument she played. It had been a stupid idea, taking music lessons from her, but it seemed so logical at the time. And as I fumbled over scales, my fingers tripping over the strings, my mother had said she'd had enough. *You're never going to be good if you fake your way through practicing, Emma. You have to practice.*

Jesus, Mom, will you stop being such a bitch? And as soon as I'd said it, I'd felt my face flush, the shame seeping into my cheeks. I'd avoided any eye contact with her, hurried into my bedroom, and slammed the door behind me. I'd sat down on my lavender carpeted floor, pressed my back against the door, and started to cry.

※

I took my father's car over to Annie's that night. It was an old Volvo, with a navy cloth interior, and the smell of coffee was thick in the stale air. The car was cluttered with papers everywhere, a stack of photocopies in a couple of piles on the passenger seat. I turned the CD player on and something folky floated through the speakers. I didn't know who it was; it sounded a little like the Grateful Dead. When I was a kid, my father would give me a quarter if I could correctly identify the music playing in the car. Once, when I was eleven, he gave me five dollars because I knew it was Fleetwood Mac before Stevie Nicks joined the band.

I'd never felt so accomplished.

On my way over to Annie's, I felt slightly calmed by the drive—by the smooth, even pavement, the empty roads, the Christmas lights looped around people's trees. I'd always loved driving through these neighborhoods that time of year, past the colorful lit-up homes, the ones whose roofs were lined with mazes of red and green lights. I got to Annie's just a few minutes later; her house was at the end of a cul-de-sac, with a wide sloping lawn that was covered with that kind of hardened snow that crackled beneath my feet.

Annie threw her arms around me at the door. She was wearing plaid pajama pants and a Columbia sweatshirt; her hair, long and wavy, was swept up into a bun.

"I'm so happy you're home!" she said.

"Me too, me too."

"Henry's just in my room. Can we go hang out there for a little? Is there anything you wanted to do tonight?"

"No, this is perfect," I told her. "I'm tired, had a long day, long drive."

"Oh right, obviously."

Henry was lying on Annie's bed with a TV remote in his hand, scrolling through the channels. He had shaggy brown hair and his face was unexpectedly scruffy.

"Hey, Emma. Welcome home."

"Henry!" I leaned over onto the bed to give him a hug and play-fully rubbed his hair, which had grown so long since the last time I'd seen him. Henry and Annie had begun dating right after I'd left for Oak Hill. Annie liked to joke that this was precisely why they'd got-ten together, but I knew it wasn't really true. We had all been friends since middle school and I think he had been vaguely in love with her the entire time. He was quiet and thoughtful, had an understated sort of humor. In the ninth grade yearbook, he was voted "Talks Least, Says Most," which was precisely the sort of person he was.

In a way, Annie and I had always monopolized each other, ful-filled every role and function in each other's lives, and so it was only fitting that it would take me leaving to allow room for somebody else. By October of that year, she and Henry had fallen into a sweet and comfortable romance.

"What have you guys been watching?" I asked.

"Nothing," Annie said. "We've just been staring at it and waiting for something good to come on. We were watching *Breaking Bad* before but it was getting too violent for me."

"I love that show but sometimes I just can't stomach it," I said.

Henry was rolling a joint on top of one of Annie's old yearbooks. I watched as he ground the weed between his fingernails and deli-cately arranged it onto the slip of rolling paper. Afterward he twisted it up and sealed the edges with his saliva.

Annie and I had smoked weed together for the first time, in ninth grade. It was the Wednesday night before Thanksgiving, and we were hanging out with a boy named Ethan who had a crush on Annie. Some of his friends came over and we all piled into his big walk-in closet, which was immaculate for a fourteen-year-old boy; his jeans and khakis hung neatly over wooden hangers, hooded sweatshirts and colorfully emblazoned basketball jerseys displayed as though in a sporting goods store. Ethan passed me the joint and I held it cautiously between my fingers. I looked at Annie for the okay but she just smiled and shrugged her shoulders in this carefree sort of way that was so unlike either of us. I held the smoke there in my body for as long as I could before coughing, doing my best not to heave dramatically. Afterward, when the boys seemed sufficiently high (laughing so much that they claimed they were about to "piss their pants"), we watched a movie and Annie and I sat on opposite sides of the couch texting one another, trying to figure out if it had worked. *Maybe? Kind of? How do I know?*

"Do you want some?" Henry asked me now.

"Yes!" I said, emphatically. "I haven't smoked since before finals. Can we just smoke in here?"

"Let's go to the basement," Annie said.

In seventh grade, her parents had renovated the basement, gutting the old wood-paneled walls and ceiling, adding a jukebox (always aglow in pink neon light) and a huge, arcade-style Pac Man game. It was the site of a lot of activity in those middle school years, with a pullout couch and half a dozen air mattresses blown up on the carpeted floor; Annie's friends and I would stay over whenever we could, savoring our first real taste of privacy, a little space sealing us off from the rest of the world.

We walked past the den, where both of Annie's parents had fallen asleep, even though it was only ten o'clock. Her father was on his back, on a brown leather couch, and one arm dangled off, grazing the carpeting. Annie's mother was sitting in an armchair, her feet resting on an ottoman. Her reading glasses had slipped into her lap, the magazine section of the *Times* beneath them.

"Your mom got a haircut," I whispered. "She looks so cute."

Annie and her mother had the same beautiful red hair, thick and glossy. They had always looked so much alike: striking green eyes, pale skin, and a constellation of freckles across their rounded cheeks. Their genetic composition was all exposed, their lineage mapped out for everyone to see.

When we got to the basement, Henry lit the joint, the tip a hot ball of amber. He inhaled a couple of times, and then passed it to me.

"You guys," I said, "my mom was being so, so weird tonight."

"Weird how?"

"I don't know, just crazy."

"Can you elaborate?" Annie said.

"Something was just off. It was like she was suddenly senile or something. I don't know how to describe it."

"What kinds of things was she saying?" Henry asked.

"She was just confused about everything. She was paranoid, saying someone had stolen her clothes even though they were obviously right there. It was insane." I took another hit of the joint.

"Maybe she was having a reaction to something?" Henry suggested. "Is she on any medication or anything?"

I turned to Annie. "He is so thoughtful," I said. "Admit you have the best boyfriend."

They both laughed. "Yeah, I guess I like him?" Annie said.

"But really. You're so lucky. Daniel barely listens when I talk to him." (This wasn't entirely true and I wasn't sure why I'd even said it.)

"I can't tell if you're already so high or you actually just think that. And that's not even true, Emma. Daniel's great."

"He is. I mean obviously, he is. He's wonderful. But we wouldn't be friends, you know? Like if we'd all grown up together, he would have been friends with the girls who played lacrosse and thought we were artsy freaks because we wore Converse, and skirts over our jeans."

"We *are* artsy freaks," Annie said.

"No we aren't! I hate when you say that. Plus, you cannot implicate me any longer; you're on your own in that place now." I lay down on the beige shag rug. The floors were heated; I'd always loved that about Annie's house. I wanted to lie there forever. And then I moved my arms and legs together and apart, made fake snow angels into the plush ground beneath me.

"I miss this house so much," I said. "You don't know what I would give to just be here, all the time. And now that my mom is insane I probably will be."

"She's not insane, Em. I'm sure everything will be fine."

"I should go home soon."

"Are you too high to drive?"

I considered this for a moment. "Um, maybe?"

"I can drive you home."

"But what about my car?" I said.

"I'll drive your car and then Henry can follow and we'll take my car back.

"He's barely high anyway," Annie reassured me.

"No, no, that's too much." I sat up. "I'm fine. I'm high, but I can drive."

"But you know we hate that," Annie said.

"It's cute that you guys 'we' each other so much," Henry observed. "Annie, you never do that with us, only with Emma."

"Well, it's different," Annie said, and smiled at him, kissed his hand. "'We's take years."

"It'll happen, Henry, don't worry," I said. "One day she'll be 'we-ing' you left and right."

※

ANNIE drove me home a little while later. It was only a two-mile trip and there were no highways, just two big intersections and then across Mamaroneck Avenue. I was zoning in and out, feeling the warm leather beneath my hands, thinking of Daniel. And when we got to my house, I was so relieved, so grateful I hadn't driven back there by myself. The moon was full and pale, completely unobscured against a black, black sky.

"Thank you so much for driving me," I said. "I'm so happy to be back here."

"I'm so happy you are too," Annie said.

Henry pulled up behind us.

"Okay and I hope your mom's all right, by the way," Annie said. "I mean, I'm sure she is, but just keep me posted, okay?"

chapter
3

ON Sunday, I took the Metro-North train into the city and then two more subways to get to Daniel's. It felt a little less frigid there, a little less windy, as if somehow all the light, the people, the city brimming with activity, could generate a kind of warmth.

The doorman stationed in front of Daniel's building smiled at me. "27P?"

"Yes, thank you!"

The elevator opened directly into their apartment and Stella, Daniel's chubby Maltese, was waiting at the door. She panted and her mouth hung open in a way that seemed impossible not to interpret as a smile.

"Hello, little girl, hello!" I told her.

Daniel walked out shirtless, wearing boxers that said "Daniel's Butt Mitzvah" across the back. He kissed me on the lips and pulled me gently down the hallway.

"You're naked," I said accusingly.

"We have the heat way up."

"Wait, wait! Should I take my shoes off? It's so slushy outside."

"Oh sure, whatever you want."

"Are your parents home?"

"Not yet, soon. Patrizia is making dinner, though. They should be home in like half an hour."

I'd been to this apartment a half dozen times, but I was still somewhat amazed each time I got there. The ceilings were so high and there were floor-to-ceiling windows, a patio that wrapped around half of the twenty-seventh floor, overlooking green stretches of Central Park, where the reservoir—silver and gleaming—sat in its center. But then Daniel's room was nothing out of the ordinary; it could've been any seventeen-year-old's bedroom anywhere. Posters were taped to his walls—Wilco, the Walkmen, Neil Young. And in the corner, he'd started drawing with what looked like charcoal pencils; it was the beginning of something, two figures embracing. Maybe it was naive of me, but at the time I sometimes thought that if I'd had an apartment like that, I would've felt compelled to keep my room nice, to make my bed every morning and organize my books and not leave all my clothing in piles on the floor next to my dresser. But maybe I was wrong, maybe your bedroom was always just your bedroom, no matter how wealthy your parents were.

Daniel's parents were doctors—Jane a psychiatrist and Steve an internist. Both of them had private practices nearby, and Steve was on the faculty at Mount Sinai Hospital. Every so often they took trips to countries in West Africa, flew out in a tiny plane, set up little makeshift clinics for a week or two, but never stayed long enough for the reality of the despair around them to settle in, and, perhaps, permeate their own first-world lives.

When Jane came home, we all walked into the dining room and she embraced me warmly, pulled me close, and a slew of bracelets clanked together as she rubbed my back affectionately.

"Sweetheart, it's so nice to see you again!"

Steve smiled and lifted his plastic, thick-framed glasses up on top of his head. He was handsome in a conventional sort of way that my father wasn't, with a thick head of silver hair, and striking hazel eyes. "Have a seat. We're not so formal here, if you haven't noticed."

"So, Emma, I remember you told me you were having some anxiety about leaving your hair iron plugged in on the carpet every time you left your dorm room. Is that still worrying you?" Jane said. She was sitting across from me and wearing a tank top, with lots of cleavage exposed. Her chest was tanned and freckled, ornamented with a bulky turquoise necklace.

I laughed, a little embarrassed. "Oh! I don't know? Not really. I guess I haven't used it in a while anyway." There was something so disarming about how candid Jane was, and also something utterly likable about her openness and the way the entire family just seemed to home in on what they really wanted to talk about.

"You guys look tan!" I said, doing my best to change the subject. "Where did you just get back from?"

"Oh, I go to this little salon on Columbus Avenue every now and then," Steve said.

Daniel laughed. "Of course you do."

"Oh please, cut it out, you guys," Jane said. "We were in Argentina. You know, Daniel's sister is over there on a Fulbright. We had a wonderful time, really. Lots of delicious food."

"So, Daniel," Steve interrupted, "you just plan to hang out at home and bother us for a month? What are you going to do here until you go back to school?"

"I was thinking tonight that I was just gonna buy an ounce of weed. That should last me a little bit? Should be pretty blazed and happy, and stay out of your way."

I cringed at hearing Daniel say the word "blazed" in front of his parents, but his father didn't seem concerned. These were the kind of parents whom you could talk openly to about anything; they were free of judgment and welcomed any sort of conversation, no matter how awkward or inappropriate.

"An ounce!" Steve said. "I don't think that'll last you too long. But seriously, you're here for almost a month, right? I think we ought to get you an internship or some sort of volunteer position? Do you need to start visiting colleges?"

"Steve," Jane said, "he just got home! Leave him alone, he's on vacation."

"Vacation from what? From taking four classes and smoking marijuana with his friends and reading a little here and there? That's hardly what I'd call hard work."

"That's really all you think I do?" Daniel said.

"Well, I'm going to call Ralph and see if he has anything you can help out with again. Okay?"

Daniel turned to me. "So, my dad went to college with Ralph Nader and he never actually votes for him but likes to maintain this pseudorelationship with him, so he can pretend he's still liberal."

Steve sighed and laughed a little. "It's complicated, okay?"

"We live in a two-party system, blah blah blah. A vote for Nader is a vote for Bush, for McCain, Romney, whatever. Doesn't that sum it up?" Daniel asked.

"Basically."

"Sorry to interrupt," Jane said, "but what kind of wine do we want with dinner?"

"Anything red. I'll get it." Daniel got up from his seat and examined the bottles of wine encased in a glass cabinet on the other side of the kitchen. I could feel my face flushing just a little, could feel myself filling up with affection for this family. There was something so sophisticated about them, the way Daniel's parents seemed to regard him almost as their equal. Would my parents *ever* have asked me what kind of wine I wanted? Would I even have *known* the answer to that? I felt a swell of desire as Daniel walked back to the table, a slim, dark bottle in his hand. I was so relieved to be there with him and his family, after feeling so constricted at home. Every so often I felt a flutter of panic about my mother. Though I'd barely seen her the past couple of days, something still seemed so off. I kept thinking about asking Daniel's mother for her professional opinion about what was going on, and I had this fantasy about telling her each and every detail of my mother's odd behavior, imagining that somehow Jane would have an explanation for everything, and I'd be calmed by her maternal and medical wisdom. But I'd somehow convinced myself that my mother was probably okay, that I was probably overreacting, as I often did.

We finished dinner and a couple of glasses of wine, and then moved over to the living room. I folded up in a corner of the couch, cupping a stemless glass in my palms. Jane told a story about a trip their family had taken to Paris when Daniel was about seven or so. He'd been extremely attached to his blankie and had it with him throughout the vacation, bringing it along to the Louvre and the Left Bank, and every other tourist attraction they visited.

"So, the moment we get on the plane," Jane continued, "Daniel has a panicked look on his face that says, *where is Blankie?* I assured him it was in our luggage underneath the plane and we'd find it as soon as we landed. He's a little skeptical but he believes me, I guess. But you know, we never did find the blankie—we looked and looked and I even called the hotel when I got home, but it never showed up."

"Mom, you're taking way too long to tell this story," Daniel said. He drained the wine from my glass.

"Do you see how he picks on me?" Jane asked.

"Do you see how great she is but how long she takes to tell her stories?"

"Okay, okay. So days, weeks go by. Then we get the phone bill at the end of the month and it's unbelievable, I mean, through the roof! Turns out we have all these calls to France."

"You're kidding," I said.

"Daniel was calling the hotel, every day. He'd come home from school and just call the concierge and hang up!"

"Oh, you're so cute," I told him. "How did you even get the number? And why were you hanging up?"

"I don't know how I got the number—I guess I was just a resourceful little kid. I was just expecting that someone would pick up and tell me Blankie was there! Or that Blankie himself would pick up."

"That is *too much*." I was a little tipsy, my lips stained with wine. I loved him. I had never said it out loud, but I knew that I did. I felt overcome with it for a moment, watching Daniel with his mother, their easy laughter together.

Afterward, both of us a little bit drunk, we went into his room and I got into bed. That we were allowed to sleep in the same bedroom was something of a novelty—at school it was impossible, and my parents wouldn't have been comfortable with it either. Daniel's parents didn't even seem to consider that it was an issue—perhaps it was the double standard of him being a guy, or maybe they were just so evolved and open-minded that it simply didn't bother them.

Daniel fumbled with his iPod, which was connected to big boxy speakers on either side of his room. He put on some Neil Young album—and this was something I really admired about him: he played full albums at a time, the old-fashioned way. No singles, no iPod mixes, just the whole record, straight through. Daniel had always been serious about music, but not in an annoying, dogmatic sort of way. He'd told me he just felt that the structure of his favorite albums, their order and cohesiveness, were all deliberately and very carefully planned. And I understood—it was something my father would've said too.

Daniel got in bed beside me, brushed my hair away from my face.

"You know, my dad thinks I'm just this boring stoner who doesn't care about anything. It's not true. You *know* it's not true."

"Oh, I know," I said, and I climbed on top of him, straddled my legs around his waist. "I'm not so worried about that."

❋

I got back to Westchester midafternoon. It was one of those strangely beautiful days in winter when the sky was a single stretch of blue, untouched by clouds, the sun gleaming and bright, despite the icy weather. I walked into the foyer of my parents' home, which opened up directly into the living room, and saw my mother standing barefoot on the couch, a roll of silver duct tape in her hand, lining the edges of the window with thick strips of adhesive.

From where I was standing, it almost looked as if she were decorating the room for a birthday party or some equally festive event, almost as if she were one of those crafty mothers who taped colorful signs to doorframes and filled rooms with shiny, congratulatory balloons. But there was something hurried in her movements, something frantic.

"Mom?"

"Yes?" She sounded exasperated.

"What are you doing?"

"I'm sealing the windows."

"From what?"

"Can you come closer? I can't really hear you."

I went into the living room, sat down on the leather loveseat across from the sofa my mother was standing on, kneading her bare toes into the plush cushions.

"Sealing the windows from *what*? Dad already put in the storm windows when I was home for Thanksgiving."

"No, no, no! I'm not worried about the cold. It's just that we need to be careful."

"Careful of *what*?"

"Emma," she said, and she ripped a piece of tape with her teeth, pulling at it, twisting her neck to the left. "They put bad things out there and sometimes you just have to protect yourself, okay? They put toxins in the air and I don't know why, I can't tell you why, I wish I could, but I can't."

I stared at her. At the slight creases below her eyes, which made her look so tired, exhausted, really. I didn't know what to say.

"Who's 'they'?" I asked her, but she ignored me.

We sat in silence for a minute and then she continued, "Someone is trying to hurt us and I just want everyone to be okay. I'm just trying to make sure that none of it gets through the windows. I already sealed my bedroom and I'll do yours when I'm finished here."

"Does Dad know?"

"Know about the poison?"

"That you're sealing the windows."

"Well, I didn't start until he was at work today. I've tried to explain this to him before, but he doesn't really seem to understand the severity of it."

"Are you feeling okay? Do you feel sick or something?"

"Oh please, please, *please* don't do that. You think I'm crazy, Emma? You think I'm crazy because I want to protect my family? Do you think I like living this way? Living in a home that could poison me at any minute! This is torture, *torture* for me!"

❄

THE rest of the afternoon passed slowly. I didn't know what to do. I wondered if I should call 911 or my father, or maybe just Annie or Daniel, someone to talk to. But really I didn't want to do any of those things. I didn't even want to move, just wanted to let this uncomfortable feeling in my chest settle. I went into my room and closed the door behind me. My bedroom had barely changed since I was a kid: purple carpeting, pale pink walls, a white, faux-wood desk that still had the faded remnants of Magic Marker scribbled on the drawers. (I'd done this when I was eight or nine and then my mother and I spent an entire Sunday afternoon trying to scrub the desk clean, using various kinds of brushes and sponges, soft, plain ones and Brillo pads with thick, wiry backs. Nothing would do; after all these years, there was still this faint writing, which now seemed an oddly sweet artifact of my childhood.) AMME DNA EINNA was still visible in loopy, faded, peach-colored writing. It was something of a fad then, in third grade, to write your name backward, and it had seemed like such a feat when Annie and I were able to write *both* of our names backward *together*. For months we'd written notes to each other this way, imagining that no one could understand our secret, coded language.

I tried to distract myself by reading Gawker, browsing Facebook, looking through whole albums of people I barely knew, checking to see what my roommates had been up to since we left school: one of them was in Turks and Caicos with her family; another was skiing in Vail. She posed next to her younger brother—they looked breathless and wind-burnt in big, heavy parkas. The semester had only been over a handful of days, but already a senior guy had been "asked to leave" (this was the prep-school way of getting expelled) because he stayed on campus a few days after finals and was found drunkenly passed out in the evergreen shrubs behind his dorm. There was a whole thread of Facebook comments, people writing to say how unfair it was, how they wanted to protest the administration at Oak Hill. I tried to care, to focus on anything other than my mother, but it wasn't working.

I lay on my bed, flat on my back, and tried to steady my breathing. Okay, so yes, I *should've* called someone, but earlier in the week when I'd mentioned to Annie and Daniel that something was off, I hadn't meant it like this.

My mother always had an abundance of neuroses, but none that had ever seemed to verge on psychotic. She always made me unplug the toaster oven after I used it, and sometimes she'd come into my bedroom in the middle of the night to peel my socks off because she worried my feet would be too sweaty while I slept. She was always fastidious about washing fruit, even grapefruits or tangerines, when the skin was simply thrown away. It didn't matter if *I* was the one eating it and didn't care about the potential harm of pesticides. We had fought about these things mercilessly at times, and thinking about it now I could feel the tension rising in my chest. *You're being so crazy,* I would scream at my mother. But obviously that wasn't really what I'd meant. I'd meant neurotic, controlling. I'd meant, couldn't she just leave me alone for five minutes and let my feet sweat if I wanted them to?

I had only been home for seventy-two hours and somehow everything seemed different, irrevocably warped, having shifted in the cruelest way.

Maybe I would go to the movies. Maybe being in the dark, in an empty theater, sealing myself off from this bleak time of day, when afternoon leaned toward darkness, would be just the distraction I was looking for. When I was a child, I used to call dusk the loneliest time of day. And at seventeen, I still felt the slightest bit unsettled as I watched the sun sink into the sky.

I wondered if it was possible to sneak out of the house without having to engage in another lengthy, distressing conversation with my mother. And as I slipped out the door a few minutes later, I could hear her muttering to herself, rearranging some furniture in the den, shifting the coffee table this way and that.

chapter

4

MY father was sitting in the den with a book in his lap when I returned. The lights were off, and the scene seemed so stilted, like the beginning or ending of a play.

"Dad, why are you sitting like that in the dark?"

"I don't know. I came in here to read but I guess I just forgot to turn the lights on and got a little distracted."

"LIT?"

"Hmm?"

"Lost in thought."

"Ha, yeah, I guess. Mom and I got into a fight while you were out. She left a couple of hours ago and I haven't heard from her. Her phone's off."

"Did you call Aunt Elaine?"

"Yeah, she's not there."

"How worried are you?"

He sighed heavily, closed the book in his lap. "I don't know," he said.

The landline rang a few minutes later. It was a call from the manager of the A&P down the street. He said there was a woman sitting at the loading dock. She was okay, but seemed a little disoriented, a little confused. Her ID said she lived at this address. Did someone want to come by?

It was a six-minute drive to the A&P and we were totally silent as we made our way there. My father usually loaded some CDs into the stereo or chose a playlist from his iPod before we went anywhere, but that night we arranged ourselves quietly in the car. No music, no NPR, just the soft ticking of the turn signals, the wheels against the icy pavement, the quiet hiss as the heat floated through the vents. I was thinking of things to say, a legitimate question I could possibly ask, but nothing felt appropriate; everything seemed either too dramatic or sentimental or too frivolous for what was happening.

There was a pounding in my head; my eyes were glassy and wet.

"I'm so confused," I finally said.

My father didn't respond, just slammed the base of his hand against the steering wheel, honked at the guy ahead of him, who had stalled at the light.

"That wasn't meant at you," he said, turning to me for an instant. "Sorry."

The shopping center was nearly empty. There were a couple of SUVs parked here and there, and a tiny Honda hatchback that looked decades old. At the other end of the lot was a Best Buy, its bright yellow lettering luminous against the dark, starless sky. And there was my mother sitting on the pavement, just beside the loading dock of the supermarket. Her hair was short and choppy, mostly dark but speckled with gray. From the distance she looked like a child, a little boy waiting for someone to get him, to bring him home.

She was dressed in the same outfit as earlier in the day—dark jeans, leather flats, a navy cowl-neck sweater. She was wearing a down jacket that was unzipped, and no hat or scarf or gloves. She'd always hated winter accessories. As we got closer, I could see that something in her face looked strange, a little off, her eyes focused on something in the distance. She seemed calm, though, without that frenzied affect she'd had earlier. I turned away, didn't know where to look. I felt as though I might be sick and I wondered if this was the moment that I'd look back on and know, irrefutably, that everything had changed. I wished that I could've somehow held onto and savored the ordinariness of the past few days.

❅

MY father carefully approached her, then squatted down to her level.

"Carol, you need to come with me," he said gently. "It's too cold for you to be sitting out here like this. We're going to get you some help and then we're going to head home." He was firm, but had adopted the same sort of tone that I used when I was babysitting for some sweet but unruly five-year-olds who just wouldn't get to sleep.

"Look, I told you yesterday that it wasn't safe anymore," my mother said. "I know this is hard for you, but I just can't do it. They're going to kill me if I stay there. You have to believe me. It's just not safe."

"Carol."

"I know you don't believe me or understand, but I'm okay here, really, I am. You don't need to help me."

"I don't need to help you? Carol! This isn't a joke. Listen, we'll take you to the hospital and get your meds readjusted and then you'll be fine. Please. Please don't do this!"

My mother laughed in a dry, sardonic way and then said, "Oh stop, he just doesn't know any better."

"Just stop," my father said. "Please just stop responding to *them!*"

"Dad, seriously, what the fuck is going on? Should I call an ambulance?"

Someone from the store, a young guy, his face ablaze with acne, was standing nearby. He was wearing green khakis and a starched red shirt with the A&P emblem on the left side of his chest. His hands were clasped behind his waist.

"Do you mind giving us a minute?" my father asked him.

"Oh, of course, I'll be right inside if you need me."

"It's supposed to snow tonight, Mom," I said stupidly, as if this kind of logic might be helpful. The air was brisk and icy, and I just stood there, next to a clump of dirtied snow and a dip in the pavement that was filled with a pool of slush. I stared at a few empty, flattened potato chip bags, watched as a lone can of Diet 7Up rolled away and disappeared.

"Emma, I need to take care of this, and I think you should go home," my father said.

"Are you kidding? I'm not gonna just leave you here."

"Emma, please, I'm serious. Call Annie or your aunt or someone, and tell them to pick you up. Now."

❄

I waited for Annie's car to pull up, and I thought about how much time we'd spent in this parking lot before I'd gone away to school, smoking cigarettes and leaning against cars, waiting for something interesting to happen. I kept imagining the moment when I could tell this story—tomorrow or next week or next month—and say, *It was so terrifying, it seemed like my mother was totally losing her mind, but then it passed, it was all okay.*

Annie arrived in her father's sleek gray coupe. Each seat had its own temperature dial, and she had set mine one notch below the highest, the way I'd always requested it. I could feel the heat seeping in through my coat, and something about that small act of intimacy, of Annie's thoughtfulness, made me start to cry.

"Thank you so much," I told her. "But I can't . . . Is it okay if we don't talk right now?"

"Of course, of course. Whatever you want. We'll just drive back to your house." The windows were all fogged up from the cold and I dragged my fingers along the glass, drew ribbons and shapes in the moisture, like I'd always done as a child.

When we got home, Annie hugged me again and unloaded the backpack she brought filled with DVDs and a couple of magazines from the checkout aisle at CVS. When we were thirteen, we went to this party at a tenth grader's house, and I accidentally got so drunk I spent an hour upstairs in the bathroom crying, trying to will myself to throw up. Annie just sat there with me on the ceramic-tiled floor, rubbing my back, promising me everything would be fine. And something about the certainty in her voice, the calm, soothing way Annie had spoken to me, made me want to believe her.

I wanted, so badly, for her to do that again.

"What the fuck is happening, Annie?"

But she couldn't this time, didn't have much to offer me. "I don't know, I really don't."

❅

AS soon as I got into bed, I called Daniel, but he was at a party and it was too noisy to talk and could he call me back later? I texted him instead: *Something really crazy is happening with my mom. Can you call me back?*

He didn't call for forty minutes and by the time he did, I was too angry or sad, my insides too twisted up, to answer the phone.

❅

THE next morning, everything was still and quiet. I'd gotten a text from my father just after six A.M., letting me know that my mother had been admitted to the hospital in White Plains, and I should come by whenever I got up. I lay in bed for a while, trying to force myself to move. I was expecting to see chaos—as if the house would somehow physically reflect the senseless disorder and confusion of the past twelve hours. I was expecting the living room to look like the aftermath of a tornado that had swept through—broken glass, garbage strewn everywhere, a badly soiled carpet. But when I left my bedroom, I saw that the kitchen sink was clean and polished-looking, a handful of forks were upright in the drying rack, some books were stacked neatly on the coffee table. Our family cat, Grandpa, was stretched out, resting sleepily on the sofa. A roll of duct tape sat beside the windowsill, and a strip of silver hung limply, like day-old confetti.

I took a shower and called Daniel, who sounded half-asleep and was too hungover to talk.

"Hey, baby," he said. "My head is killing me. Can you just call back a little later?"

"Ugh, no. You're so annoying! Do you want to talk to me or not?" I had never spoken to Daniel this way before, but suddenly I didn't want to be polite, I didn't want to have to act my best around him anymore.

"Jesus, do you have to be *so* dramatic, *all* the time?"

❋

I was sitting in the county hospital, in the waiting room, in the psych unit on the ninth floor, where my mother had been admitted just a few hours earlier. The walls were painted a pale shade of green and there were matching pleather chairs and a television in the corner that was running a loop of the same few news stories. I heard someone say, *Your dad is not bipolar, he has bi-polar disorder.* I thought about that difference, and I stared at the woman who was uttering these words, at the two inches of exposed sock between her loafers and her black dress pants. The woman was wearing Garfield socks and I stared absently at the cat's face—bright and bloated like a pumpkin, set beneath a thought balloon with a piece of lasagna and a clutter of *zzzs.*

I waited there for what seemed like forever, while my parents met with a team of doctors, and I made a tally of all the bad things I'd ever done: in seventh grade I stole two cigarettes from Annie's father, on my fifteenth birthday I made out with Evan Berger even though my friend Rachel had given him a blow job the week before, and I'd cheated on my algebra final in ninth grade.

I thought about these things over and over again. I couldn't stop running down the list even though I understood, on some basic level, that none of this was related to what was happening to my mother, that none of it made any difference at all. Eventually a nurse came out to report that my mother was in the day room, and that I could follow her there. I looked up and saw my mother through the Plexiglas square in the middle of the doors—just the top of her head, her eyebrows, the wisps of her brown hair. I felt something sickening in the back of my throat, hot and sweet and burning, and just like that I threw up all over the floor, the lime-colored linoleum tiles suddenly splattered with puke.

❄

AFTER having waited so many hours in the hospital, the visit with my mother was only a few minutes long, cut short because an obese man who looked like he was in his thirties had begun screaming, shrieking, really, and two guards rushed over to restrain him. They ended up having to lock down the unit and all the visitors were forced to leave. But for those few minutes, my mother and I sat in some sort of day room, which was lit up in an oddly hostile, aggressive way. There were no windows, only bright yellow beams of light that lined the ceiling. A few plastic tables and a dozen or so plastic chairs, a stack of board games piled up in a corner—other than that, the room was empty.

My mother and I barely spoke. She looked like she was going to cry—her jaw tense, her eyes wet—but she never did. She said hello, in a soft, tender voice; she said it twice, three times, maybe, but other than that she was silent. She was looking at something, but I didn't know what. I stared at my mother's feet, which rested in thin, turquoise paper sandals. I was thinking about a time in the late nineties: it was Passover, my family was having a seder at my grandmother's house in Queens. I remember wanting something, but I don't know what. Matzo ball soup? More orange juice? Maybe just some water. My mother had been talking to someone, engaged in conversation, but I had been impatient and really wanted her attention. I pulled at her hand, tugged at her thin, unpolished fingertips. And then I looked up and saw that it wasn't my mother I'd been pulling at, but her sister, my aunt Elaine. I thought of that momentary feeling of horror, the hot slap of embarrassment and shame, when I looked up and saw only the absence of my mother. Never mind that it was my mother's younger sister, someone who so closely resembled her, who had the same fine, permed brown hair, who wore the same simple diamond ring on her finger—but none of it mattered. All I could think was, *This is not my mother.*

※

WE'D driven to the hospital separately, but instinctively I followed my father out into the parking lot, opened the passenger door, and sat down beside him. He stuck the key in the ignition and flipped it forward just an inch, and then a handful of red dots glowed from the dashboard, and the radio emitted a soft, blurry static.

"Look," he said, "she's going to be okay, I promise. She'll stay here for a little while until she gets stabilized, but then she'll come home and things will be all right."

"Okay." I sat with my tote bag on my lap, the cotton handles twisted snugly around my fingers.

"I know this must be really hard and really confusing."

It occurred to me then, in that moment, that there was something about my father's calm, the ease with which he was talking to me, that suggested this wasn't new to him. I wondered, suddenly, if my mother had been psychotic like this before. But when? It didn't seem likely. I wasn't an idiot; wouldn't I have known if my mother were crazy? If she'd always been this way?

"Yeah. I *am* feeling a little confused, I guess," I said.

"Okay, well, do you have any questions?"

"Can you turn off the radio? Or change the station or something? What *is* that?" There was a hostility in my voice that I hadn't shown to my father in years, since middle school, maybe.

"Sorry, sweetie." He pushed in the dial. "So, what do you want to know exactly?"

"I don't know! I don't even understand how we're having this conversation. I mean, everything was totally normal until three days ago, and now you're acting like I've been living on another planet this whole time. I just really don't understand what's going on."

"Look, Mom's had some mental health issues. She'd been fine for so long. You know she's been in therapy."

"Everyone is in therapy! That's not a thing." I felt like a child, here with him in the car, as if my year and a half away at school had meant nothing, the independence and sophistication that I imagined I'd been nurturing were meaningless, gone. But I couldn't help it, didn't want to help it.

"I know, just listen to me." My father pressed the tips of his fingers against the steering wheel, leaving momentary indentations in the leather. "She's been in therapy and on medication for many years. And every so often this happens, every so often there's a little break. She just needs to get stabilized again and maybe change her medication a bit and find a good . . . a good combination."

"How is it possible that I've *never* known about any of this? That just seems crazy." Was this part of the reason why my parents had been so invested in me going to boarding school? Had my mother been steadily losing her mind for the past couple of years and they'd wanted me out? To protect me from witnessing exactly what was happening right now?

"Look, there hasn't been anything that you've needed to know. She hasn't been hospitalized since you were really little. Everything has been fine for many, many years. She's been stable for over a decade!" My father's voice cracked. There it was—the tiniest bit of grief. Sorrow. I had been pressing him but I'd pressed too hard.

"And what was it before that? Before she was stable, what was wrong with her?"

"Schizophrenia."

It had begun to snow. I felt grateful for the easy distraction—and so I just stared ahead, focused my eyes on the flakes as they landed on the windshield and dripped down the glass.

"She was first diagnosed when the two of us were seniors at Tufts," my father said. "We'd already been together for two years . . . She was struggling a lot, but she was somehow able to keep things together, and then she went to the hospital right after graduation. She was there for a long time. A month or so. It was a hard time, but slowly things got better, you know? The drugs weren't as good then, but they worked with some heavy side effects. This was when we were living in Boston. She got a job with a small newspaper in Brookline and after a couple of years things seemed totally back to normal. We knew it was there, this thing lurking behind both of us, but we were happy. She was healthy. And we got married in the fall, and then we waited another few years to make sure that things were fine, and really they were. And we consulted with lots of doctors to make sure that it would be okay to have you. All of them said the same thing: that if she was closely monitored and went off her medication for a little bit, but stayed in therapy, in a supportive environment, low stress, things would be okay. And they were!"

"And then?"

"This is a lot to take in and a lot to talk about," my father said. "Maybe we should just go home and keep talking in the morning?" He scratched gently at his beard.

"Just get to the bad part, okay?"

"This is it, this is all of it."

"Yeah, but you said she was hospitalized when I was a kid."

"Right, when you were about four. She needed to get things readjusted, find some sort of equilibrium again."

"How long was she there for?"

"About ten days."

"Did I freak out?"

"You were okay. You were a tough little girl. And you went and stayed with Grandma for a little while."

"And things have been okay since then?"

"Yes, they really have." He paused. "Let's go home, Emma. Do you want to leave your car here and we can just drive back tomorrow and get it?"

I nodded my head yes. I worried that if I started to speak again, I would begin to weep. I hadn't been so openly upset in front of my father in years. I pressed a knuckle against the radio dial and then with another couple of taps, the CD player lit up. Bob Dylan's voice, raw and scratchy, filled the car.

❋

WHEN we got home, I lay in bed and tried to gauge exactly how dumb and naive this new information made me. Was I like one of those sixteen-year-old girls who went into labor without even knowing that she'd been pregnant? It seemed impossible to not feel something growing inside of your body all those months, to willfully ignore all those hormones shifting. Would people look at me and wonder the same thing?

That night, I couldn't sleep. I started by just typing "schizophrenia" into Google, and hours later I was still awake—lost inside the endless maze of mental health sites, message boards, virtual support groups. The information was abundant and terrifying. I typed in, "My mother has schizophrenia" and the searches that automatically filled the search bar were "My mother has schizophrenia, will I get it?" "My mother has schizophrenia, do I?"

I looked up the symptoms: delusions, hallucinations, disorganized behavior, thought disorders. I wasn't sure if I knew what it all meant. What was disorganized behavior, exactly? Did the fact that I was messy and often careless—that every winter I lost two pairs of gloves, left a scarf wherever I went—count as disorganized? I didn't think I had hallucinations—that didn't worry me much—but then I read further: *auditory hallucinations*, hearing voices. This left me slightly confused, a little on edge. I didn't hear other people talking to me when they weren't, but wasn't there always a voice in my head? Narrating my every move? Was that normal? Did everyone have that?

I typed in, "famous people with schizophrenia." I wanted to see public figures who had suffered in this way. The list was shockingly small. I was hoping it would be the kind of thing where half of the artists and writers I admired were actually plagued with the illness, but probably, I'd been thinking of bipolar disorder. After an hour of googling, all I could come up with were Brian Wilson from the Beach Boys, Syd Barrett from Pink Floyd, Jack Kerouac, and Ezra Pound.

I went back and reread the symptoms. I started to feel panicky as I read. Whatever slight curiosity or uncertainty I'd started out with earlier in the night had been replaced by a persistent, definitive terror. I was crazy too, or if I wasn't now, then I would be soon. I tried to calm down. I reminded myself of the time sophomore year when I convinced myself that I had herpes. I'd spent an hour in the girl's bathroom on my hall, staring at myself in the mirror as I'd been taught to do by the sex ed teacher. I didn't know if what I was looking at had always been there, was my normal skin, or if I had recently contracted some disease. I'd gone to student health later in the day, after I just couldn't take it anymore, and the nurse practitioner looked at me like I was an idiot. *Dear, you're totally healthy. There's nothing wrong; it's completely normal down there.* I closed my legs and hopped off the table. *Great, thanks.*

But this seemed so different. You either had herpes or you didn't, right? I googled the average onset age of schizophrenia for women and it was twenty-five, which left me feeling both relieved and more anxious; I had eight years left.

chapter
5

DANIEL was sorry, he said, really, really sorry. This was over the phone, and he wanted to come out to Westchester and talk. He said he hadn't realized the extent of this crisis with my mother. He took the train out early the next day, but for some reason I just didn't want him to come over, to be in my parents' home, which still felt like something of a crime scene.

I picked him up at the train station in White Plains, and when I saw him, I felt a brief flicker of tenderness. I'd been so cold and unloving toward him the past couple of days, but the warmth of his body, the faint smell of his breath as we kissed hello that morning, and I felt myself softening toward him. The tips of his hair were still slightly damp from his morning shower, and I squeezed a handful of it.

We went to a diner close to the station; it was one of those twenty-four-hour restaurants, but in the morning light the neon sign was faint and pale against the gray sky.

"Wanna do the sweet and savory combo?" Daniel asked, holding the tall, laminated menu in his hands. Sometimes when we went out for breakfast, I'd get eggs and turkey bacon and he'd order French toast or pancakes, and we'd split the food half and half.

But I shook my head.

"I'm just gonna have coffee," I said. I *was* pretty hungry, and wouldn't have minded sharing breakfast the way we usually did, with some fluffy eggs and crispy bacon. But it just didn't feel right, and I didn't want Daniel to think that this was going to be an ordinary breakfast, a normal meal.

"So tell me," he said. He pushed the menus to the side and held on to my hands. "Tell me what happened."

And mostly I did. I told him the basics: that my mother had had a psychotic break, that she was suffering from paranoia and would be in the hospital for who knows how long. I didn't say that this had happened before, didn't reveal that sense of embarrassment and betrayal I felt at never having known this fact about my mother (a fact that seemed so crucial to her identity, so relevant to the very essence of her being). It was not precisely a lie, but a muddled, more comfortable version of the truth.

Daniel moved over and sat down next to me on my side of the booth. The vinyl was ripped and smoothed over with tape beneath us. He took one of my hands. "I'm so sorry, Emma."

I knew he was; he must've been, but what else was he thinking? There were so many thoughts and anxieties circulating through my head, and I shut my eyes and started to fake a cough but really I began to sob. I let it all out, but tried to muffle my cries into Daniel's shoulder. He kissed the top of my head.

"It's okay," he said. "Look. Emma, you know I love you, right?"

I nodded my head yes, said, "I think I do?" We both laughed a little at that.

"I do too," I said. "I mean, I love you too."

✳

IN October, just a month after we'd started dating, we'd gone to his parents' house in the Berkshires for a long weekend. It was sixteen hours of driving, just to be there for a couple days, but we'd had Monday off for Columbus Day and decided to make the trip. It was the sort of thing both of us liked to do—to travel long distances to be somewhere for just a short period of time. It was also the sort of thing that my parents would've said was ridiculous, a waste of time and especially gas, but I didn't really care and had just told them I was staying at school for the weekend. I felt almost dizzy with excitement at the thought of us alone in the country house together—I would've driven twenty-four hours just to be there with him for a single night.

We left school after class on Friday afternoon and drove through much of the night. The roads were so empty it seemed we could go hours without seeing a car in the other direction, just the blank, dark sky, the horizon low around us. It was unseasonably cold and even in the car I wore a big knit sweater and plaid scarf beneath my coat. I loved fall, loved it even though it was chillier than expected. I loved the burnt and fiery smell in the air, the trees shedding their skin and piles of leaves ornamenting the street corners. That time of year always made me feel wistful, and there was something especially romantic about spending it with Daniel.

It was a big, old house with green-trimmed windows, set on two acres of land. Inside was all exposed wooden beams, and it had a sort of rugged but polished feel. The downstairs was a large open space; up above was a balcony that held all of the bedrooms. The furniture was spare, and there was no TV (this was on principle, Daniel had said—his parents were adamant about it), but there were lots of bookshelves, a long oak table, and a wide island in the center of the kitchen. In the living room was a mahogany baby grand piano, and I felt a pang of jealousy on my mother's behalf, knowing just how much she would have wanted this for herself.

Daniel brought me upstairs to the attic, which his parents had turned into a library. The walls were lined with built-in shelves, filled with medical books and journals, and some old fiction as well, lots of dusty brown spines and yellowed paperbacks. I thought of my parents' house, which was filled with books too, though I couldn't ever imagine my parents being able to refer—with a straight face—to a room in their house as a library. But in a way my mother's books *were* a library to me. I loved combing through them—all the old Russian fiction, and whole collections of contemporary writers: John Updike, Philip Roth, Margaret Atwood, Alice Munro. Sometimes I would take books down from the shelves, not always for the sake of reading, but to skim through my mother's penciled marginalia, which were always there. I just loved the idea of it—being able to trace back her thoughts, her little comments—some as simple and benign as *"oh!"* or an underlined sentence here or there.

❋

THE pantry had been stocked with lots of basic, non-perishable food, so we mostly cooked soups and pasta (lots of mac and cheese), and made sandwiches with peanut butter and a loaf of sourdough bread that had been packed into the freezer. We shared a bottle of red wine and sat on the living room floor and played cards: rounds of spit and bullshit and gin and rummy. By the end of the night, we were drunk and my fingertips were pink and numb.

We slept together in Daniel's old twin bed, beneath a bright orange-and-blue Mets comforter. We were still learning about each other's bodies, what worked and what didn't, but that night I felt aglow with pleasure each time Daniel moved his hands or his mouth; every subtle gesture brought me closer to coming. And eventually, we both did, just at the same time, and once that rush of feeling subsided, I'd wanted so badly to tell him that I loved him. The urge snuck up on me so unexpectedly I literally had to cover my mouth in fear that the words would slip out. Over the next few days, I'd been waiting for one of us to say it; even though I knew we hadn't been together long—just over a month—it seemed as though we might be ready.

But that morning, at the diner, as my hands rested on the table sticky with syrup, all of that waiting somehow felt like forever ago. When Daniel said that he loved me for the first time, I didn't feel giddy or light-headed as I might have felt that weekend in the Berkshires. All I felt was tired, and sad, and just a little relieved.

✳

IT was clear and cool on the Monday afternoon when we had driven back to school from the Berkshires. Somewhere near the Connecticut border, we'd gotten off the highway to stop for gas and get a quick bite to eat. We were at a big intersection, with a handful of fast food restaurants to the east and a sprawling K-Mart to the west. We were stopped at a light when we were abruptly jolted forward, hit from behind by a bulky SUV. And then we had slammed into the car in front of us, too. The SUV hadn't been moving that quickly, but still there was enough force for the rear bumper of Daniel's Subaru to detach and hang limply from its base, and for me to smack my forehead hard against the dashboard.

"Fuck!" Daniel said. "Fuck! Are you okay?"

"I'm fine, I'm fine." I touched my fingers to the spot above my right eyebrow, discovered it was damp with blood.

"Shit, Emma!"

Daniel got out of the car to examine the damage. A stout, dark-skinned woman in a sari rushed over from the SUV, apologizing profusely.

"I'm so sorry!" she said. "I got a call from my sister that she's in the hospital and I just got distracted! I'm just so worked up and worried and I just wasn't paying attention!"

"It's okay," Daniel said to her. "It happens. Everyone's fine, don't worry, let's just call 911 and exchange our information."

❄

I needed three stitches but was otherwise fine. The emergency room was nearly empty, and Daniel sat in the plastic seat beside me, resting his hand on my leg as the doctor closed the slit above my eyebrow, still caked with blood.

"Wait until my dad hears that we got into an accident because you were giving me road head! He'll be pretty pissed!"

"Shut up," I said. I could feel myself blushing. I tried not to move, careful not to disrupt the doctor's hands. "You aren't funny."

"Well, I'm *a little* funny," Daniel said.

❄

AFTER the pain and shock had subsided, I still felt a little shaken up, emotional, really, and the first person I wanted to call—as I usually did in situations like this—was my mother. And then I'd felt shitty about not having told my parents I was going away to begin with, and hoped that they wouldn't be angry. (*You're seventeen,* Daniel had said. *You don't have to call your parents every time you make a move.*) I wondered if I shouldn't even call, but I always felt anchored by my parents in circumstances like this, soothed by the idea that they would do whatever they could to ease my anxiety. My mother was always so composed, so calm in situations that made me panic.

I called home and choked up just at the sound of her voice. (Why did this always happen? Why did I always regress to a five-year-old when I was in touch with my parents and even the tiniest bit distressed?)

"Oh sweetie pie, what is it? Is everything okay?"

"Yes, yes, I'm fine, sorry. I'm totally fine." I wiped my nose with the back of my hand. "Daniel and I just got into a little accident. I'm okay, but I just feel kind of shaken up and wanted to call you."

I remembered this moment at the diner with Daniel, as he cut through a stack of pancakes, and I wondered if I would ever again be able to rely on my mother. For anything at all.

chapter
6

MY father was on his winter break from school too, and so for the next eight days, we were both free to roam the open spaces of that strange, dark time. Free to indulge, to pick and dissect, to really embrace all that darkness. I wished so much that things had been different, that instead, we could both be overwhelmed with a thousand different things, constantly coming and going, running into each other briefly at the hospital, trading duties, exchanging information about my mother, her moods, her medication. I'd say, *Oh they upped her Seroquel five milligrams today* and he'd tell me that she seemed more like herself, even asked for the Arts and Leisure section of the *Times*. But the reality was a little different. He was home a lot— spending a lot of time reading, sitting at the computer, engaged in something, though I wasn't sure what.

We had never spent this much time in the same place without my mother. Once, when I was in third grade, she went to visit her friend Andrea, who was living in San Francisco at the time. They had grown up together, and Andrea was the only person my mother still kept in touch with from elementary school. It was only a long weekend—three or four days at the most that she was gone—but I remember those days clearly, how much I missed my mother, how I could never quite loosen up in the presence of my father, and how, unless I was thoroughly distracted, I'd be on the brink of tears, and could have cried at any moment. My father had planned a lot of activities for us that weekend, mostly arts and crafts related; we built igloos out of sugar cubes and melted broken crayons together to make rainbows to draw with. But my mother had left me notes around the house, index cards cut in half where she'd written that she loved me and that she'd be home soon. They were tucked beneath my pillow or beside the breadbox in the kitchen. She traced her hand on a piece of purple construction paper and told me, *Whenever you miss me, you just hold on to my hand, okay, sweetheart?* Each time I was reminded of her, could feel the faint presence of her in the house, I would feel awash in longing again, overcome with despair.

And now, being alone with my father, I was just as uneasy, but this time it felt different, as though it was some conscious decision on our part, as if we'd chosen to team up against her, chosen to leave her stranded in that strange, cold hospital.

※

THE next morning, the sky was a pale open stretch of gray, the kind of day where it seemed like maybe it wouldn't ever rain. Before we left for the hospital, my father asked me to help him pack a suitcase for my mother. He sounded annoyed. "We should have done this days ago," he said, and he lifted a black rectangular suitcase from the top shelf of the closet.

"How long are we packing for?" I asked.

"I don't know, really. A few days?"

He grabbed some bras and underwear from my mother's dresser—one of those old, cherry wood sets of drawers, with antique brass handles. Something about watching my father, his callused hands fumbling around with those delicate bras, felt so uncomfortable. A small peek into a life that I didn't want to see.

"A pair of jeans?" I said. "And a sweater or two. That gray turtleneck, and the purple cardigan she always wears."

We packed more: a pair of Reeboks (in a plastic bag so that the soles wouldn't dirty the rest of her clothing), a couple of books—a new Anne Tyler novel and *Best American Short Stories*—a little jar of face cream that she applied dutifully every morning, one set of flannel pajamas from the Gap.

When we got to the hospital, a security guard stood beside the elevator on the psych floor. She had a long ponytail that trailed down the center of her back, rested just below her waist.

"Come over to this table," she said.

My father set the suitcase down as she requested.

"Well, firstly," she said, "you know you can't just come in here with a suitcase. We'll open it up and go through each item one by one." She unzipped the bag and opened the flap. "And no plastic bags, either." She took the sneakers out of the bag and set them on the table. I stared at her nails as she sorted through my mother's things—they were painted a bright, glossy red, except for her two ring fingers, which were forest green and decorated with tiny dots of silver and gold.

"Little trees," she said, catching my look. "Just trying to stay festive in this damn place."

"They're cute," I told her.

"Look, sweetheart," she began, and it seemed she was talking to both me and my father, "you guys can carry these things in yourself or you can get a paper bag downstairs. And you can bring the sneakers but I have to take the shoelaces out. And no hardcover books either. And not this lotion, sorry about that. No glass." She was matter-of-fact, methodical, as she set the contents of the bag on the table beside her, separating them into two different categories.

"These are fine," she said, gesturing at the pile of clothes and one hefty paperback.

Inside, the hall was actually decorated warmly—doorways were strung with red and green beads, tinsel was draped over the long oval desk at the nurses' station, and one of those plug-in plastic menorahs ornamented a waiting area. That year Hanukkah fell early and was over by the second week in December, but the menorah was still there, the elongated orange bulbs lit up dully. All of a sudden I felt so grateful that we didn't actually celebrate Christmas. I imagined how much more depressed we'd all feel that day if we were missing out on some sweet family tradition. Daniel's father was Protestant, and though Daniel had a bar mitzvah and went to Hebrew school for nearly a decade, his enthusiasm for Christmas was palpable. He'd spent the last month at school ordering presents online, compulsively checking eBay, bidding on rare books for his father or signed copies of his sister's favorite albums. I rarely saw even the slightest hint of sentimentality in him, but there were a handful of traditions for which he felt a lot of affection. That night his family was throwing their annual Christmas Eve cocktail party, and Daniel told me they'd hired a caterer and a string quartet to accompany their carols. It all sounded so nice, but I just didn't know if I'd be able to go, be able to stomach all that festivity.

※

WHILE my father was talking to the doctor, I walked into the common area and saw my mother in there by herself, pacing the room's short length. Her feet were padded in thick, gray woolen socks, and I worried she was going to slip on the linoleum floor; something about her gait was a little off. She looked different than she had a couple of days before. More alert, less dazed, her hair combed, the buttons on her sweater properly aligned. I wondered if they'd given her some sedatives the other day that had now worn off.

As soon as she saw me, she said, "You have to get me out of here. I mean, this is ridiculous. You know I don't belong with these people. I was just trying to protect you, protect us, our family. This is crazy!"

"Mom."

"Please, Emma! Don't do this to me. Please, please, I'm begging you. I'm asking you very seriously. I'm asking you nicely. I can't, there's just no possible way that I can stay here."

＊

I thought of Visiting Day the first summer that I went to sleepaway camp, almost a decade earlier. I had been so desperately homesick and remembered begging my parents in a calm, tempered way. Like if they only understood how absolutely impossible it was for me to stay there another month, they would then have no choice but to bring me home with them.

I had never seen my mother like this. And in denying her what she so desperately wanted, I felt as if I were being forced to do the cruelest thing any daughter had ever done. I felt like I couldn't breathe, like I was choking, or worse—that I was choking *her*.

"This is too much," I said.

"I know," she whispered. "But please, Emma. I know that you understand me. We've always understood each other in a way that other people don't. Daddy loves me, I know he does, and he's a wonderful father, but it isn't the same, he doesn't understand. I know that you can help me, please." There was an urgency in her voice, but it was slightly dulled, a muted version of how she'd been in the house that day, frenzied and a little wild, ripping strips of silver duct tape with her teeth.

I swallowed, clenched my teeth so that I wouldn't cry. "I can't. I don't know what you want me to do. I just don't have any choice in the matter."

"But you do, sweetheart. Just explain to Dad that I don't need to be here. Please. I'm begging you." She brushed my hair out of my face. We hadn't touched in days and her fingers were freezing. I didn't mean to, but I flinched just the slightest bit when I felt her fingertips skimming across my forehead.

"And if you're not going to help me," she said, and her voice was so icy, "you'll have to leave."

I got up and left, didn't even try to argue with her.

※

LATER, my parents were in a conference room, meeting with a couple of doctors and the social worker. I sat cross-legged on a bench in the hallway, and even though the peach-colored blinds were pulled down, I could see my mother through the slits of plastic. I started to wonder if there was any way that she wasn't delusional—could she possibly have been right about poison seeping into our home? It was unlikely, yes, but it was still plausible. There were crazy, malicious people, *sociopaths*, living in this world, and maybe my mother was on to them. But immediately, I wondered if my willingness to believe her was proof that I was headed toward that same kind of psychotic thinking. Could I somehow be persuaded into madness?

※

MY mother looked like a defiant teenager in there, her face turned away from the doctors, her hair slick with oil, tapping her fingers impatiently against the plastic table. I thought about whether or not

I should go to Daniel's party, and in a way, I felt desperate to get out of there, to get away from my family, yet it also seemed so clearly the wrong thing to do. If my mother were in an ICU, if she had breast cancer, leukemia, MS, would I go to the party tonight? I tested myself with each disease and ailment I could think of. I imagined my mother hooked up to wires, tubes snaking in and out of her flesh, her eyelids waxy and swollen.

❄

MY father dropped me off at home while he went to see his brother, who lived in Riverdale, not too far from us. All the lights were off in the house and a cool blue was slanting through the windows. Grandpa walked in between my legs, brushed his tail up against my calves. I picked him up and held him like an infant, cradled him in my arms. "What do we do?" I asked him. I was crying and I whispered into his face, pressed my lips against his fur. *What. Do. We. Do.* He blinked, jutted out his little pink tongue for a moment, and let out a tiny sneeze.

I put him down and went into my bedroom. I started to change my clothes, put on a pair of dark gray leggings and a long sweater that I liked to wear as a dress. I took a lighter out of my underwear drawer (this was where I kept everything bad: condoms, a tiny bag of weed, matches, lighters, a cloudy glass bowl with yellow streaks like lightning bolts down the center). I rolled my thumb against the little metal wheel and clicked the piece of plastic, and a sliver of flame erupted, orange and bright. I lifted up the leggings on my left leg and pressed the fire against my ankle. I flinched for a second but then I put it back.

My skin was burning.

I felt a wave of extraordinary heat but after a moment it stopped hurting and for the first time in days I felt deeply calm. So at ease with myself and everything around me. I closed my eyes, felt the warmth against my skin, my breath slow and heartbeat steady.

※

AFTERWARD, I finished getting dressed and went into the bathroom. I rubbed a dot of Neosporin on the spot of my skin that was bubbling up, becoming a blister, and carefully covered it with a plastic Band-Aid. I told myself it was okay for me to go to the party because here was the evidence of my pain, my love for my mother, right there: hidden on my left ankle, a little swollen patch of purple skin, tender and sore.

※

I drove the car into the city, sped down the Henry Hudson and then south on the West Side Highway, the river black and choppy alongside me. The radio stations were all playing Christmas music and I sang aloud to the ones I knew—that Nancy Sinatra song, and some old Mariah Carey cover that I loved. There was no traffic; the city felt empty, and I glided off the highway, headed east on 96th Street. Broadway was lit up, the trees on the mall were all studded with yellow lights, bold and bright. I parked easily just off Columbus, turned off the car but sat for a moment before I got up. I rolled up the bottom of my leggings, lifted the plastic bandage to check on my wound, puffy and pink, a little swollen. I stroked it delicately, careful not to pop the blister. In the rearview mirror I applied some eyeliner, which always made my eyes look more green, less brown, and added some lip gloss. I put my hair up and then took it down again. I was always pale, but I looked paler than usual tonight, and I pressed a dot of lipstick on each of my cheeks, smoothed them in circles on my skin.

※

UPSTAIRS, the apartment was brimming with people. I headed straight to Daniel's room to take my jacket off and put my bag down, and one of his friends, Kyle, was sitting at the desk. He was in a big upright leather chair, slicing through some finely ground cocaine with the side of his MetroCard. He gathered it in a single, slim line.

"Hey you," Kyle said. He put the MetroCard down. "Give me a hug, it's been so long."

"So long!" I said. I ruffled his hair a bit. "Cute haircut."

"Yeah? My girlfriend hates it. She's pissed."

"Oh, it'll grow back so fast."

"Yeah, we'll see. You want some?" Kyle asked. He wheeled the chair out from under Daniel's desk; his baggy corduroy pants dragged on the carpet beneath him.

"Maybe," I said. "Maybe just a little?"

Daniel and his city friends used drugs in a way that felt different from my public school friends—they'd casually leave a tidy pile of powder on a counter, or swallow some painkillers with a glass of tap water like it was no big deal. Yes, in Westchester, there had been plenty of weed and beer and maybe a bottle of Robitussin here and there, but it wasn't the same.

I had only even *seen* people use coke twice before, each time during the previous year. The first was with Abbe, my roommate in tenth grade. We'd had the kind of relationship that was sort of stiff and polite, but at the same time oddly intimate. During the third or fourth week of school, I walked into our dorm room and she was standing up, naked except for a striped turtleneck—cutting her pubic hair with tiny nail scissors, a pile of dark, wiry hair collecting in the center of my wastepaper basket. *Sorry*, she'd murmured, *I just haven't gotten a garbage can yet.*

And later that night, while we were both studying quietly on our own extra-long twin beds, she emptied a little baggie of coke on top of her chemistry textbook. (She offered me some in the same manner as if she were handing me a stick of Winterfresh.) It was a Wednesday, and we sat on the oatmeal-colored rug in the center of the room. She snorted a couple of lines and I just sat there and watched her, and even though I was totally sober, I was happy to match her enthusiasm, relieved at how talkative and chatty she had suddenly become. We talked of our families, how we were both pretty homesick, how much we missed our friends and the simplest luxuries of home: having a refrigerator always stocked with food, not having to share a bathroom with twenty people when we were feeling sick. It was the only time we ever really had a substantive conversation. A couple of weeks later she started dating this senior who wore tweed blazers and boat shoes and did tons of acid. He was always scaling the walls of our dorm and trying to break into the room through our window to surprise her or wake her up, and by the middle of November they were both gone.

The second time I'd seen coke was in a bathroom at some crowded off-campus party with Daniel and three of his friends. One of the day students had thrown it while his parents were away in Nantucket for the weekend. There were four of us packed inside—Daniel was leaned against the sink, and I sat on top of the closed toilet seat. Two guys were in the tiny turquoise bathtub, with their legs hanging out over the side, inhaling lines off the porcelain edge. One of them called the guy hosting the party a fag, and I looked at Daniel expectantly, like, *Come on*, but he didn't say anything, just sort of glanced at me sheepishly and shrugged his shoulders.

"Really?" I'd asked. "Did you really just use that word?" There was silence and then I wondered if I'd said it out loud, or maybe I hadn't. And I just kept hearing the word reverberate inside that cramped little room, *really, really, really*. Daniel opened up the medicine cabinet, which was mostly empty: Ibuprofen, some disposable razors, a travel-size deodorant, and an amber bottle of prescription something or other.

"Valium, anyone?" he'd asked. I felt my cheeks heating up, and my heart began to beat in this irregular, frantic sort of way. I spent the rest of the night lying in the backyard with my hand flat against my chest, listening to Annie calm me down from three hundred miles away.

✳

THAT night, Christmas Eve, I was so eager for a distraction from my own thoughts that when Kyle offered me the line, I took it. I felt the powder go straight to my head, this little tingle in my brain, and suddenly I was so alert, ready to go, eager to talk to everyone. I walked into the living room. I saw Jane, Daniel's mother, and gave her a quick hug.

"Sweetheart," she said. "Can we talk later?"

I glided through the party like the best version of myself, poised and confident, interested and friendly. I took Daniel's hand and wanted to be introduced to everyone—his grandparents, aunts and uncles, cousins from Argentina, a few of his friends from the city whom I still hadn't met.

I poured myself a glass of white wine and introduced myself to the caterers, who were dressed in black-and-white outfits with perfectly pressed crimson bowties. I had a sudden urge to tell them that I wasn't like all the other guests there, in pearls and dresses from Bergdorf, and that Daniel would never understand me, that he would never get what it felt like right then, to have my mother sequestered in a cold, sterile hospital, with tiled walls that smelled just like my elementary school cafeteria, where she couldn't even have a fucking plastic bag because they were afraid she'd use it to suffocate herself. And abruptly I saw all the flaws that were beginning to emerge in my relationship with Daniel. I knew suddenly that they were there, that it was bound to fail, that I'd go back to school and be so lonely. But somehow it was all floating past, and it was okay, as if my problems were hovering in a little bubble nearby, not touching me quite yet. For now I was happy. I took Daniel into the bathroom, the one in the hall, and pushed him down onto the toilet seat, with my legs around him.

"Whoa, whoa, whoa," he said. "What's up, baby? You pretty drunk already?"

"I'm not."

"How was your mom today?"

I shrugged. "It's whatever . . . She's whatever."

"Emma, come on. Tell me."

"I really just don't feel like it right now."

I knew that he was trying, but right then I didn't want to hear it. Didn't want to think about it. I wanted to be the girl who didn't care about anything, who was wild and fun, who could try coke like it was no big deal. I wanted to be the girl who gave her boyfriend a blow job in the bathroom of his parents' house, while family and friends milled outside the door, sipping their drinks, examining a painting that hung on a nearby wall, wondering if it was an original.

I started to undo his belt buckle, slipped the little leather knot out of its loop.

"You seriously want to do this now? My grandparents are like twenty-five feet away."

"Ugh, fuck you." I wanted so badly to lose myself in recklessness, but I just couldn't quite get there.

※

I walked into the kitchen, where the caterers were circling around each other, grabbing platters of miniature tacos with slices of sirloin steak, eggplant puff pastries, chicken teriyaki skewers. I saw Daniel's mother feeding herself a tiny potato pancake with a dot of sour cream in its center. She stopped me.

"Let's go into the den and talk for a minute?"

I was starting to feel jittery and my heart was beating heavily, pounding. I didn't need to talk, I was fine.

"Are you feeling okay? Do you want to talk? Daniel's filled me in on what's going on. It sounds like you're going through a hell of a lot right now."

I was fine. Fine. Fine. Fine.

"I'm okay," I said. "Thanks, but I really am."

She looked at me in this knowing way.

My heart was starting to slow, and I felt something else, something like emptiness, creeping in.

"Okay, sweetie. Well, I'm not going to push you, but I'm here if you need to talk. And if not me, I could find you someone else. This is serious business, okay? You need to take care of *yourself*, too."

She was wearing a chain with two gold letters dangling from the middle. *D* and *L* for her children.

"All right," I told her. "All right, thanks."

My high was coming down and I felt the faintest headache lurking somewhere in the back of my brain, waiting to rear its head. I poured a couple of shots' worth of whiskey into my wine glass and kept sipping.

❋

I woke up at five or six on Christmas morning. I was naked and felt drool caked onto the side of my face, which was pressed against Daniel's bare back. The heater was making a loud gurgling noise, and it felt like a hundred degrees inside his bedroom. I felt sick and needed some fresh air. I whispered to Daniel that I had to go, would call him later, and happy Christmas. I slipped out the door. The doorman downstairs was asleep; his eyes fluttered open and he apologized profusely at the sight of me. "No, no," I said. "Please, it's fine."

I felt awash in cold when I stepped outside. The sky was mostly a dark blue but was beginning to lighten. The street was empty, except for an old man walking a dog on the corner. She was a big German shepherd and they both walked gingerly, then the dog paused to pee, and a stream of yellow pooled on the curb beside her. The owner patted the dog's waist. "Good job, my girl, good job."

chapter
7

CHRISTMAS night, Annie and I went to dinner at an Indian restaurant in Mamaroneck. It was nestled in a strip mall where everything else was closed—a nail salon, a Hallmark store, an enormous Staples, all empty and dark. We were the only two people inside the restaurant, which had plush burgundy walls and brown velvet curtains separating the dining area from the kitchen.

"Come in" the waiter said, "anywhere you'd like," and he gestured around the open space. "Want some alone time?" Annie joked. "Let's sit on opposite sides of the restaurant."

"Never!" I said. "I never want *any* alone time." I was only half kidding. Time moved so much more slowly when I was alone, and thoughts of my mother kept seeping into those empty spaces. What was she doing and how miserable was she and what was happening inside her head? When I was at the hospital the day before, one of my mother's doctors was waiting for the elevator, her hands shoved deep into her coat pockets. She looked at me, with this sad, resigned half-smile. *Once those neurons get started*, she said, but she didn't finish, just nodded solemnly and stepped onto the elevator. I kept thinking, *Once those neurons get started*, then what? I imagined the detailed cell drawings we used to have to do in ninth grade bio, with the nerve endings reaching out, trying to connect to each other. What were those nerve endings doing in my mother's head? Were they frenzied and lost, desperate to communicate but running in dizzying circles?

※

THE moment Annie and I sat down at the table, I felt ravenous. As soon as our food arrived, I tore off big, warm pieces of naan, folded the flaky bread directly into my mouth.

"Tell me things," I asked Annie, in between bites. I was relieved by my own hunger, relieved that my body was indicating some return to normalcy. "What did you do last night? How are things with Henry?" I stirred rice into my chicken tikka masala, ate everything all at once.

※

AFTER dinner, Annie and I went into a Walgreens because it was the only place open. We roamed the aisles of the drug store, discreetly opening and smelling shampoos and body washes. We bought a pad of temporary tattoos that proclaimed GIRLS ROCK in bold lettering. There were guitars with flames, drum sets, a girl headbanging, some sparkling musical notes.

We went back to Annie's house and it was all Christmas movies on TV, except *You've Got Mail*, which was on some version of HBO. We lay down on the couch in the basement and I finally felt relaxed. Not exactly happy, but content. Annie got some paper towels and a shallow dish of water and a pair of scissors and we covered ourselves in tattoos.

"Should I make a sleeve?" Annie joked.

"I bet Henry would love that," I said.

Annie's brother, Zach, who was two years older than us and a freshman at SUNY Purchase, flicked on the lights in the basement and walked downstairs.

"No way!" Annie called. "We're watching a movie. Turn them off."

Zach had been sort of a lost soul in high school—not angsty enough for the artsy crowd but too introspective and intellectual for the more mainstream kids. He was a painter, though, and sometimes he'd come into the house a mess, broad strokes of oil paint all over his jeans. We used to joke that he did it on purpose, just to seem cool. But he'd come into his own in the past few months and seemed more at ease with himself.

He was with two of his friends that night, and he switched the lights back off and they all came downstairs to the basement. Zach sat on the couch next to me, his two friends on the carpet beneath us.

"What movie is this?" Zach asked.

"Don't pretend you haven't seen this a thousand times," I said. "You obviously know what it is."

"I know what this is," one of Zach's friends said. He wasn't exactly handsome but there was something alluring about him; he had tan skin, a long, pointed nose, inky black hair. "The one where they meet online and know each other in real life, too."

"Spoiler alert," Annie said.

The guy with the dark hair picked up one of the tattoos—an amp with musical notes coming out of it—and asked if I'd put it on him.

"Sure," I said. "Where do you want it?"

"Where do you suggest?" he asked.

I took his arm. "I like the wrist. Right here."

"Shut up, you guys," Zach said. "Tom Hanks is about to stand Meg Ryan up."

I took one of the paper towels off the floor and peeled back the thin sheet of plastic that protected the tattoo. I put it against his arm. I had no idea what his name was, but I felt this tiny charge, a current running between us, when I pressed the tattoo over his wrist, held my hand on top of it, and counted to thirty in my head. When I took my hand off, the amp was black and shiny on his flesh.

"Nice work," he whispered.

❋

ON the way home in the car, I couldn't tell if the radio was buzzing or if the heat was rattling, but there was a little noise I heard in the background and something about it was really grating. I turned off the radio for a minute and then the heat. I couldn't tell if the noise had gone away or not. And then I wondered if maybe it wasn't real at all, if maybe I'd been hallucinating. I felt this quick surge of something—anxiety, panic—in the bottom of my stomach. *Fuck.*

What if. What if. What if I'm losing it too. I tried to breathe slowly, deliberately, told myself to calm down. I put the music back on, and the heat too, and I thought the noise had gone away but I couldn't be sure, and then I didn't even know if I'd heard it in the first place.

I got home and into bed and spent the next hour googling countless variations of the same phrases. "How do you know if you have schizophrenia?" "Schizophrenia symptoms." "If your mother has schizophrenia, do you?" "Mom has schizophrenia, do I?" I found a website called Child of Mentally Ill Parents. It was one of those old sites with choppy, three-dimensional graphics and a banner that waved in slow, disjointed waves. There were pages and pages of message boards in small blue ink. I scrolled down, browsed the headlines. "It doesn't get easier, it only gets worse"; "Mom is skitz"; "Dad was institutionalized, want sum1 to talk 2."

And down at the bottom, "Feeling motherless." I opened it up and started to read.

※

DANIEL came over the next afternoon. He'd taken an incomplete for one of his classes and had to finish his final paper over the next few days. When he got to my house, he had this big yellow backpack with him, filled with his laptop and a handful of books he'd taken out of the school library before we left for the semester. He sat on my bed in his jeans and an old sweater that his ninety-five-year-old grandfather had given to him, with tiny holes along the seams. He wore these thick woolen socks that I loved.

"E. E. Cummings was such a perv," Daniel said. "I love it."

"I wouldn't call him a *perv* exactly."

"*Shocking fuzz? Electric fur?* C'mon."

"It's erotic," I said. "There's a difference between erotic and per-verted." I stood beside him at the bed and he pulled me toward him, tugged on the little belt loops of my jeans. He lifted up my sweater, pressed his mouth against my bare belly, moved his lips across the length of my stomach.

"Is this erotic or perverted?" he asked.

We kissed, but I stopped him, put the palm of my hand against his sweater.

"Would you still like me if I went crazy? Lost my shit? Ended up just like my mother?"

"I'm sorry, what?" He kissed my neck.

"I'm serious, Daniel."

"Are you? Why are you even asking me this? Yeah, I mean, sure. I don't know how to answer that. That's not going to happen."

"How do you know?" I asked him.

"Because it just isn't. You're fine."

"It's hereditary. And it's really common when you're in your twenties."

"It's not *really common*," he said.

"Fine, but I just mean, I'm seventeen, I wouldn't even know yet. It's *really common* that people find out in their twenties."

"You're okay. And I love you. Can we just leave it at that? For now?"

※

WE hadn't had sex since all of this happened with my mother. It wasn't as though I hadn't wanted to, hadn't felt the stirrings of desire—I had, it just felt complicated. But that afternoon, I felt a wave of longing, and I climbed on top of him and we undressed each other quickly but delicately. Our bodies were naked and warm together and we were totally in sync and within minutes I felt an intense release. It was a rush of two simultaneous sensations, and the instant I came I began to sob loudly, angrily. It was a guttural cry and all of a sudden I felt wild with grief.

Daniel was silent but held me tightly, and it was the best and simplest thing he could do. He moved me in a slow rock, back and forth, as my crying eased. It was grief, yes, but guilt too. I felt sick. Oddly gluttonous, as if I'd just eaten a box of deliciously sweet cupcakes with rich and fluffy frosting and was then overcome with nausea. Who fucked their boyfriend and *really, really* enjoyed it while their mother was walking around, dazed, shuffling in little blue slippers, eating anemic-looking applesauce in an overheated dining hall, in a facility where her shoelaces were taken away? I went through a list of people in my head: would Annie, would Molly from my physics lab, would Kevin who worked in the library? Would any of them?

Afterward, I went into the kitchen and took a bottle of red wine from the cabinet. I had never had a single sip of alcohol in my parents' house and I never would've done it if my mother had been around, but I couldn't possibly imagine my father saying anything, and he wasn't home anyway.

I went back into my room and Daniel and I sat on my bed, held the bottle of wine between our knees.

"All right, sir, let's focus," I said, taking one of the Cummings books from his backpack. I leafed through it and tried to find my favorite poem. I'd always claimed that I didn't like poetry, couldn't connect with it, but there was something about Cummings's lines, the simplicity of them, that I really loved. "I carry your heart with me," I told Daniel. "I carry it in my heart."

HOURS later, I woke up in the middle of the night. I felt panic in my body, a sort of tingling beneath my skin, before my mind was even alert. My heart was beating impossibly fast—as if the pounding in my chest were trying to tap out a message in Morse code, hoping to convey something urgent to my body. But I didn't know what it was. I wanted to get out of bed, but I was fearful that if I moved the slightest bit, I might upset the delicate balance that was possibly holding me together.

My thoughts ran like this: *You're crazy, so crazy, you're losing it, just like your mother, maybe you're even dying, something horrible is about to happen to you, right this very instant.*

chapter
8

MY mother was moving to a more long-term facility in Rockland County. It was privately run and apparently the nicest place that my father's insurance would cover. We drove up in the early morning, and it was almost easy to pretend that things were normal. I was in the back seat, my parents up front, NPR emitting a quiet, steady flow of news. My mother slept most of the way, rested her head against the window, and sheets of late-morning light, the brightest kind, were slanting through the glass. My father was the only one talking: he'd make some comment about the weather, the cloudless sky, the pockets of pure, untouched snow. He went on a miniature rant about Stop and Frisk, after we heard a report that three black teenagers were beaten in Brownsville for protesting when cops tried to search them. I agreed with my father, of course, but I would've given anything for him to be quiet, anything if he would, for once, stop talking about the injustices of the world and focus, for just a minute, on what was happening with us right then.

I tried to zone out. I was holding *Anna Karenina* open in my lap. I was supposed to read it for an independent study over winter break, but I'd been staring straight ahead absently for the last half hour, the same page open, and I felt a flicker of nausea each time I tried to start reading again. All I kept thinking was, *What is going to happen?* This book was so long, I had hundreds of pages to go, and I tried to imagine what my life would be like when I was three hundred pages, four hundred, five hundred in. Would I be back at school, trudging across my bleak, icy campus, or would life just slide back into its ordinary routine and my mother would come home and teach piano lessons and make pseudo-Shabbat dinners? I slid my fingernail in between some pages toward the back of the book. It opened to 524, and I wrote in tiny black letters: *this day.* What would everything be like by the time I made it to that page?

I closed the book for a moment and tried to pretend that we were anywhere else; I was a kid and we were driving to celebrate Thanksgiving at my aunt's house in Connecticut or into the city to hear the Philharmonic at Lincoln Center like we used to do. We crossed the Hudson and it was silver and gleaming beside us, unwavering, carrying on.

The new hospital had a beautiful, sprawling campus, not unlike Oak Hill or a small liberal arts college somewhere. There were a handful of stone buildings and a leafy green quad at its center. I saw staff, mostly women, huddled beneath awnings, smoking cigarettes. It was quiet, serene.

We pulled up in front of the admissions building, a little white house that was billowing heat when we stepped inside. There was smooth red carpeting and a long hallway with what seemed like dozens of offices to the left and right. I sat down on a bench inside while my parents were talking with one of the doctors.

My father was speaking much too loudly; it seemed as though any kind of talk that went on there should've been offered in something approaching a whisper. I heard him say, "We're thrilled, really, so so appreciative." He didn't know when to turn it off, didn't realize how much his enthusiasm was probably alienating my mother, though perhaps she was too far gone for that to even matter. On the walls were framed certificates and black-and-gold plaques honoring psychologists, psychiatrists, social workers. Suddenly I didn't know why I'd come here with my parents, only that my father had asked me to and I said yes. I stared at my cell phone, praying for someone to text or call me, for some sort of small distraction.

We were taken to the building where my mother would be staying—Roosevelt House, it was called—just a few minutes away from where we'd parked the car. We walked down an evenly paved cement path, wide enough for people and those golf carts that look like pieces from LEGOLAND. My mother had been silent for what felt like hours. She was almost catatonic. I wondered what kind of drugs they'd pumped her with before she left the county hospital. Her face was blank, absolutely expressionless. She was wearing one of the outfits I packed for her the other day—dark jeans and a cowl-neck sweater; from the back she might have even looked like herself.

We got to her room and it felt instantly like my father and I were dropping her off at school. We were replaying the same scene we had enacted just a few months earlier in Pennsylvania, but all of the roles were now skewed, warped into some strange, surreal tableau. The room was mostly bare and painted in neutral colors, taupe walls and a light-green plasticky dresser. My mother's roommate, Debbie, was introduced to us by one of the case managers.

Debbie looked older than my mother; she was probably in her sixties. Her hair was dark, the color of charcoal, but there were a couple of inches of silver exposed at the roots. She was wearing a navy sweat suit and tortoiseshell glasses with thick, rectangular frames. She was sitting sideways on her bed, with a book in her lap. My father, too eagerly, introduced himself and asked what she was reading.

"Oh," she said, smiling a little sheepishly. "Oh, it's nothing. Just this little construction manual. I like reading about how to build things. How to build houses, mostly."

My father smiled, nodded his head.

We both turned our attention back to my mother, who was unpacking a big canvas bag that she used to bring with her to the supermarket. Now it was filled with clothing, a small portable alarm clock, a notebook (but no pens, the hospital would provide those).

I went outside and texted Daniel. I had only been there for a couple of hours but the thought of spending the rest of the evening with my father seemed impossible. I asked Daniel if there was *any* way he'd be willing to come get me. *Long, emotional, annoying day, just want to decompress and hang.* And he said, *Of course, no problem, just give me the details.*

When my father was outside talking to someone in administration, I turned to say goodbye to my mother. Her eyes were glassy, but she seemed improbably present.

"I was just trying to protect us, Emma," she said.

"I know, Mom."

"When people try to hurt you and your family, what are you supposed to do? Just sit there and let them do it?" Her voice was calm, resigned, just tinged with a little sadness. "I'm going to stay here because it's safe for me now, for the time being, but I want you to be careful. If you can stay with Daniel or one of your friends, maybe you should do that. I know Daddy doesn't believe me, but I think you do. I think you know the sad truth about this world."

I nodded and took her hand. We hadn't held hands in years. It was such a simple gesture, but an intimacy I was no longer used to. Her skin was so dry, her fingers cracked from the cold. This happened every winter; the tips of her fingers sliced open with tiny cuts.

"I've gotta go, Mom, but I love you and I'm gonna come back tomorrow, okay? I'll bring you that stuff for your fingers. They're just so dry. Too dry."

※

I walked back to the front of the hospital. It was early evening but the sky was already completely black, the moon round and full behind a haze of yellow. It was freezing, too cold to snow, I thought, and I was so relieved when I saw Daniel's car pull up a moment later. I was about to get into the front seat when I saw Jamie, one of Daniel's friends from the city, leaning back in the seat, his hair covered in a beanie against the headrest. Jamie lowered the window.

"Want me to get in back?" he asked. "No, no, it's fine," I said, but if Daniel knew me at all, he must have known I was furious, teeming with all sorts of angry feelings I didn't know how to express or articulate. The last thing in the world I wanted was to hang out with one of his friends, let alone to have his friend know where my mother was, and come with Daniel to pick me up from this fucking mental hospital. I didn't know if I was being irrational, but I felt totally overcome with anger.

The car reeked of old weed, like stale bong water had spilled all over the interior. "It smells disgusting in here," I said.

"Well, that's nice, thanks." Daniel looked at me through the rearview mirror, gave me a quick glance.

I couldn't seem to sit still; I opened the window and the icy air was hard against my face. I sat directly behind Jamie, who pulled his zipper up on his jacket, rearranged his scarf and hat.

❋

WE got back to the city and Daniel said Jamie could get out of the car while we looked for a parking spot. I stayed in the back seat. I was waiting for Daniel to say something, to acknowledge my anger, but it didn't seem like he was going to. I was trying so hard to be passive-aggressive but maybe it just wasn't working, maybe he hadn't even noticed. We got a spot on Central Park West and Daniel climbed into the back with me. He kissed the side of my face, but I wouldn't look at him.

"What the fuck," I said finally. "Why did you bring him? Do you understand how annoying that was? Do you think I want one of your friends who I barely know coming to meet me at the hospital where I'm visiting my mom?"

"C'mon, Emma. Can you not yell? I'm sorry."

"I'm yelling because I'm so fucking pissed!" I had this childish urge to kick my foot through the window beside me. I imagined it shattering in one swift instant.

"Look," Daniel said. "I really love you but you're being ridiculous."

"I'm sorry, what?"

"You are!" He smiled this sweet smile—the smile that allowed him to get away with things his entire life. (He loved to brag about how he didn't turn in a single lab report in chemistry but somehow still got an A in the course, or how he got arrested for smoking weed in Riverside Park and his parents didn't even punish him.) "I came all the way to get you," he pointed out. "Can't you just say thank you?"

"Thank you."

"Look, Jamie and I were just hanging out at my apartment, watching a movie when I got your text. I didn't want to be rude, so I just asked him if he wanted to come with me. I didn't think it would be a big deal. Can you just appreciate it and not be a brat?"

No one had ever called me a brat before and I didn't know how carefully to weigh that comment. Maybe he was right, but mostly I just wanted him to intuit my feelings perfectly without having to say a thing. Maybe that was asking too much, I didn't know. I didn't know how to make sense of any of it. I just wanted to go home.

And as I took the Metro-North back to Westchester that night, this was what went through my head: *I hate everything. I hate my father for being able to slip so easily into the role of caretaker and heroic husband. I hate Daniel for being indifferent to my unhappiness. I hate my mother for being so lost in her own mind, so totally out of it that I can't even contemplate the idea of relying upon her.*

I had never been someone who resented other people or their happiness, but there I was, utterly alone, feeling completely isolated. Annie was doing everything that she could but it wasn't enough, and she was going skiing in Colorado with Henry's family over New Year's. I had barely spoken to my roommates since I left school last week. A Facebook message and a text here and there. I wanted to know what people did with their anger. It felt unbearable. I had no ally, and I hated my parents the most right then for not having any other children. Wasn't this precisely what siblings were for? The other day, in the waiting room at the hospital, I'd been flipping through some glossy family magazine and on the cover were blond sisters in pink snowsuits tumbling around in a clean, bright pile of snow. The text proclaimed, *Siblings: tethered for life.* And this was precisely the opposite of how I felt, so untethered, unmoored, and yet somehow completely weighed down by my own feelings.

I got home and climbed into bed fully clothed. Socks and jeans, a tank top, and one of those gray American Apparel sweatshirts, the hood pulled snugly over my head. I lay on my stomach with my knees up to my chest, my hands balled into fists. Grandpa jumped onto my bed and settled himself beside my face, delicately arranging himself on my pillow. He brushed his tiny, damp nose against the side of my face, and it was this small gesture of affection that finally made me cry.

✳

WAKING up early the next day, I felt strangely revitalized, purposeful. My mornings were usually so sluggish. I could've been in bed for at least another hour, snoozing my alarm clock for ten, fifteen minutes at a time. But that morning I felt instantly alert and ready to go. I just wanted a little bit of time alone with my mother, an hour or two at the hospital without my father and his needless chatter, his relentless cheerfulness.

I went into the den before I left and my father was sitting on the couch with the *Times* spread out in front of him on the coffee table, eating a bagel over his lap. There were seeds sprinkled everywhere— poppy, caraway, sesame, and little grains of salt all over his thighs. This was my mother's worst nightmare and for a second I thought, *Mom would be rolling over in her grave right now,* and then, *Jesus, she's not* dead. *What the fuck am I talking about?*

"Oh, look at you," I said. "Mom would be so mad!"

"What? Oh?" He looked down at his jeans and smiled. "Yeah, she sure would be. Can you grab me a napkin?" I handed him a paper towel with some kind of watercolor floral print that my mother always insisted on buying.

"I was thinking about visiting Mom this morning," I told him, "like now-ish. I'm gonna leave in a few minutes."

"Okay, are you sure? I'm planning to leave here around one or two. You don't want to wait for me, save some gas?"

"That's okay, I have plans later, but thanks." This was a lie, but I figured I'd make plans, call someone up when I was heading back from the hospital, just to make it true.

"Okay, sure, that's no problem. And do you know what you're doing tomorrow night yet?" he asked. "I know it's sort of a strange time for all these celebratory events."

"Yeah, I don't know, still figuring it out. What about you? I forget if you and Mom usually do something for New Year's?"

"For the past few years, we've been going to this little dinner party at the Friedmans'. Just a few couples, it's low-key. We're usually home by twelve thirty."

"Are you still gonna go?" I asked. "Do they know about Mom?" It occurred to me that I had no idea who knew what and who didn't, or how big a secret this all was. I hadn't talked to anyone in my family; I had no idea if my grandmother even knew.

"They don't, not yet. We'll see what happens in the next few weeks, how long her hospital stay will be. I might go tomorrow and say your mother is sick. I don't know, I need to think about it. Oh, and I keep meaning to tell you, my friend Peter and I are going to the synagogue to do a soup kitchen for New Year's Day, for brunch, if you're interested. It's just a few hours, serving food. It's a really nice thing."

I thought about New Year's Day last year. My mother had invited her friend Andrea over for brunch since she was in town for the holidays. Andrea and my mother had both skipped fifth grade, moved directly from fourth to sixth together, and had quickly clung to each other and become best friends. She was a foot taller than my mother, muscular and big-boned with wide shoulders like a swimmer, and I imagined them wandering their Queens junior high school together, Andrea guiding my mother down the hallways, through throngs of classmates who were only eleven or twelve, but who to my mother, impossibly tiny and only ten, probably seemed infinitely older.

I'd helped my mother prepare brunch for Andrea before she arrived, arranging baby carrots and cherry tomatoes on a little tray, mixing sour cream and a Lipton soup mix to make onion dip. I cut up slivers of red and yellow peppers, while my mother made a frittata with spinach and mushrooms. This was not something I would have ordinarily done—hung around while my mother had lunch with an old friend—but since going to boarding school, I found myself longing for these sorts of cozy, familial activities around the house. Just spending time with my mother as she cooked, standing beside her in our warm kitchen, wallpapered in yellow tulips, the satellite radio set to the classical station that she loved, this was what I wanted.

"Thank you for helping me, sweetie," she'd said, and she adjusted the timer on the oven, though I knew when I walked into the den that she would probably rearrange the vegetables herself, fixing them a bit more gracefully on the teakwood tray.

Andrea arrived, and her presence seemed to instantly change the air in our mellow home, illuminating it with a burst of energy. She had three sons and was always yearning for some kind of antidote to all that testosterone.

"My girls!" She threw her arms around my mother. Her hair was past her shoulders, thick and the color of wheat. We stood at the doorway and she hugged me, saying, "You're getting so freaking old I can't believe it!"

"Come on in, let's sit," my mother said.

We seated ourselves at the table and Andrea fawned over me in a way that was slightly embarrassing, but I could see the pleasure my mother took in it, the pride—that glint in her eyes as she rubbed my back or pulled my long hair away from my face.

"Tell her about school," my mother said. "This place is pretty incredible, Andrea. I mean, if Emma could see what our high school was like, with all the linoleum and those tiny little wooden desks and those teachers who were totally disinterested, and five hundred people idolizing the football team. Oak Hill seems like paradise."

"You're so lucky," Andrea said to me, and then she turned to my mother. "But I couldn't let her go away if I were you. Even with my boys, smelly and grumpy, and their sweaty, disgusting soccer uniforms smelling up my laundry room. Even with all that, I couldn't let them go!"

"It's not easy," my mother said. "Believe me, it's not. I start to cry every time she leaves, but we're good about talking a lot, several times a week. And it's just such a good opportunity for her; she'll go to college and it will be a breeze for her, and she's so much more sophisticated, even now, than we were at her age."

"Okay okay," I said. "Can you stop talking about me like I'm not here?"

"Sure, so tell me how sophisticated you are, Emma," Andrea said, smiling at me.

"I'm not! I don't even know what she means."

"The classes she's taking, they're just so wonderful. World history, sure, chemistry, sure, but these electives—Fellini and the Italian Cinema, The Role of Women in Fascist Germany, a whole class on Tolstoy! It's remarkable, really. And she's only a sophomore. Can you even remember the classes we used to take? They were mind-numbingly boring."

"So boring we didn't even have to go!" Andrea said.

"Excuse me? My mother, the most dutiful and diligent student, didn't go to class?"

"Oh please, it was just senior year. I'd already gotten into college. I was still a straight-A student!"

"I'm shocked!" I said.

"Don't be too shocked," Andrea told me. "It's not like we were taking LSD or anything, we would just cut school and stay at your grandmother's house all day and smoke cigarettes and play Scrabble.

And your mother would argue with me over this word and that; it was nothing too exciting."

Later, I went into the living room to watch TV—to zone out in front of some MTV countdown. I could hear Andrea and my mother talking and then abruptly breaking into hysterical laughter, and I remember being suddenly hit with the realization that my mother was just an ordinary woman, a person with friends, gleeful to be reunited with Andrea, the way I would be if I hadn't seen Annie for months.

It was only a year ago! I felt an ache of sadness thinking about it; it seemed like such a recent memory, such an ordinary one, really, and in some ways attainable, and yet it was in the past and could not be gotten back.

chapter
9

MY mother was in the middle of a group therapy session when I got to the hospital that day. I waited for her on a bench in a wide, open corridor, the walls decorated neatly with framed photographs of serene, majestic landscapes—they looked like they might have all been Ansel Adams prints, the sort that were often collected in glossy calendars or used as generic screen savers. This place was infinitely nicer than the other hospital, less sterile and terrifying—not the kind of place where horror movies were filmed, where people ended up murdering each other, or nurses poisoned their patients—but it was still a hospital. Patients walked around in this slow, lethargic way, their feet shuffling forward. Every so often there was a shriek and a scuffle. Security guards emerged quickly and then were gone.

While I waited for my mother, a man walked toward me and for a moment I couldn't tell if he was a patient or staff member. He had cropped salt-and-pepper hair and wire-rimmed glasses, but as he got closer, I could see he had something red caked on to the front of his

Oxford shirt, something thick and shiny that resembled fake blood. Maybe it was ketchup or cranberry sauce.

"Are you here to see me?" the man asked, squinting as he approached me. "Did someone send you to visit me?"

"No, no, I'm waiting for my mother."

"Are you sure?"

"Yeah, I'm sorry."

"They said someone was coming to see me," he insisted.

I shrugged my shoulders, tried to smile in an apologetic sort of way.

"People don't come nearly as much as they say they will. Can you imagine what that's like? Your family throws you into a place like this, thinks because they're pouring in the money they can just leave and you'll be all set. It's a horrible thing, horrible. You know I was a real family man, in my time. I had a job, provided for my family in all the ways men are supposed to do. I made furniture, beautiful pieces of furniture, oak tables and desks. I sanded them down myself. Not like furniture these days that's shipped from who knows where, made by Chinamen or some kids in a factory. This was American, handmade. It was beautiful. I had a wife! Two children. Three, really, but one of them didn't make it. Died just a week after she was born. Anyhow, you wouldn't believe how successful I was, really."

I imagined he would go on and on with his sorrowful autobiography, but a moment later my mother appeared. She looked exhausted and weak, her veins pronounced like a faint blue subway map beneath her skin. It seemed almost impossible that I had seen her just the day before. Her hair was so greasy, and this was what she would have hated most. Throughout my childhood she was fastidious about washing her hair and mine. *Squeaky clean*, she used to say. Once or twice when I was a kid and she had a stomach virus or the flu, this would be the first thing she'd mention: *My hair is so greasy, don't look at me!* But now this was clearly so far from her mind.

We went into the dining room, which was being set up for lunch. There were a couple of people playing cards at the table next to us. One of them had his back to me, but the other guy, whose face I saw, looked so familiar, though I couldn't place him. There was something about his eyes, the slope of his nose. He was thin, so thin that his cheeks had that sunken look to them. He was a patient, I assumed, and he was wearing a dark gray sweatshirt that was zipped all the way up. He had the same absent stare as my mother, that overmedicated kind of look. As if all the life had been drained out of him. I tried to imagine what had brought him here—maybe he swallowed a handful of pills or had some kind of delusional mania where he was convinced he was a prophet and spent days in a row preaching to his imaginary followers until he finally surrendered himself to the hospital.

"Hey Ted, it's your turn," I heard the guy with his back to me say. "You all right?"

"Yeah, uh-huh." He stared at his cards, fanned them out in front of him, and then the visitor, whoever he was, stood up and walked over to the back of the room where a handful of people were preparing food and asked for a cup of water. People were removing Saran wrap from trays of vegetables, carrots, slices of peppers, and cherry tomatoes. I caught a glimpse of his face as he walked back toward the table. He nodded at me, shot me a look that was something like complicity.

It was Zach's friend. The guy from the other night, the one whose wrist I held for thirty seconds while I was applying the temporary tattoo onto his skin. The patient must have been his brother; they looked so similar, and yet they were totally different versions of the same gene pool. Zach's friend was tanner, thicker, fuller, a more fleshed-out, lively rendering of his brother.

My mother and I made small talk. I asked her about her roommate. I told her things that she didn't care about, benign details about my life that she had once been so eager to hear. I told her that Daniel and I had gotten into a fight the night before, and I was feeling so distant from him; that Annie and her boyfriend were doing really well and that she just went to Colorado with his family; I told her that the Joyce Carol Oates essay we liked in the *New Yorker* was actually part of a memoir and that it just came out and I was excited to read it.

She had barely been responding to anything I was saying, but then she looked at me. "I had to stop reading the *New Yorker.*"

"How come?"

"It's complicated, but they were sending me messages. Coded

warnings in 'Talk of the Town.' We don't have to get into it now. It's over, anyway. The instant I come into a place like this, they stop. They know I don't have access to anything interesting in here anyway. Anything remotely intellectually stimulating."

"I can bring you things," I told her, ignoring the rest of what she had just said. She'd been so checked out, so lost in her own thoughts that I hadn't even imagined she could possibly be bored. "I'll bring you books next time I come. What would you like?"

"It's fine," she said dismissively. "It's fine, but thank you, that's sweet."

I noticed earlier that there was a piano in one of the day rooms and I asked her if she'd be interested in playing.

"I am," she said. "I think I want to do that."

"Have you asked the social worker if you can? I'm sure they'd let you. I mean, I assume that's what it's here for."

"The subject hasn't come up."

"Let's make sure we do that today, before I leave, okay?"

I looked up, and Zach's friend was walking toward me. I told my mother I'd be right back.

"Hey," I said. "Tattoo guy."

He smiled. "Yeah, that's me. Phil."

"This is so bizarre. Is your tattoo still on?"

He laughed and lifted up a sleeve of his flannel shirt. "A little bit, yeah,"

"Is that your brother?" I asked. He hesitated. "Sorry, you don't have to answer that."

"No, it's fine," Phil said. "Yeah, it is. Twin brother."

"Wow."

"What about you?"

"My mother." I gestured toward her.

"When did she get here?"

"Just yesterday. What about your brother?"

"A while. It's been a few weeks."

"How's he doing?"

"Eh, he's all right. Getting there slowly, maybe?"

"Well that's something," I said. "I should go back to my mom, but it was really nice seeing you, considering everything."

"Yeah. Maybe we can drive up here together or something?" He asked. "You live right near Annie and Zach , right?"

"Yeah, pretty close."

"Are you on winter break for a while?"

"I am, yeah. A couple more weeks. What about you?"

"Like ten days," he said. "Here, give me your number and I'll just call you so you have mine. I try to come out here every day, every couple of days."

I gave him my number, then felt the belated buzz of my phone in my back pocket.

"Cool," he said. "I'll be in touch."

I was half expecting my mother to ask a million questions when I walked back over to her. *Who is that guy? How do you know him? Where did he grow up and what school does he go to?* I felt a little deflated when she didn't, though I shouldn't have

been surprised. She was barely awake anyway, her eyelids flutter-
ing open and shut.

✳

MY aunt Elaine arrived at the hospital just as I was leaving. We almost passed by each other in the parking lot, but she spotted me as
she was getting out of her car, called out to me above the gleaming
roofs of SUVs. As she and my mother grew older, they had begun to
look less and less alike. Elaine's hair had grown long and was impec-
cably styled, sleek and straight, without a single strand of gray.

"Emma!" she called, and then she rushed over to hug me,
grabbed on a little too tight. "How is she? How are *you*? And how is
your father doing? I've barely spoken to him the past few days. We
keep missing each other. He's been such a mensch though, he really, truly has." It was a quick flurry of questions and remarks, which
was a relief, really, because it seemed as though I wasn't actually
expected to answer. Elaine tapped a button on her keychain, and
the headlights on her car flashed twice, in quick succession.

"I want to take you out to dinner soon," she said, holding on to
my hands. "One day after all the holidays are over and things have
settled a bit? I'll come to Westchester or we can meet somewhere in
the city. We'll figure it out. We can do something nice, just us girls."

"That would be nice, thanks."

It was bitingly cold—Elaine's cheeks turned red and my nose had
started to run. Dozens of yellow leaves skidded past us in unison, like
dancers who moved swiftly across a stage.

"I should head back," I said, "but Mom will be so glad to see you."

"Thanks, sweetheart. I'll call you soon, okay? I promise. One night next week, your choice."

I checked my e-mail before I started to drive and most of it was nothing, spam or Facebook notifications, but there was also an e-mail from Jane, Daniel's mother.

Hi Emma, I know you're going through a really difficult time right now and I sense that you're being very brave and mature, but I would still like to take you out to lunch, sometime soon. Please. Think of it as a favor to me. You let me know when you're free. Xx.

I could feel the way these women were reaching out to me, and I knew that in some sense they were trying to fill that maternal void. But I didn't know quite what to do with it, if I even wanted that space to be occupied at all. Maybe I needed to feel the ache of my mother's absence, for at least a little while. I put my phone down, promised myself I'd respond to Jane another time.

It was the middle of the day as I drove back to Westchester. My fingers were freezing, and with my free hand I cupped my palm over the heating vent, felt it seeping out against my skin. My head was clouded with this vague sense of dread, but I didn't know how to tease the feelings apart, dismantle and separate them, analyze them like I usually did. It was all too close, too soon, and impossible to pick apart.

At home, I texted Andy and Josh, two of my friends from Westchester who I only really talked to when I was back home during school breaks. They were a couple of years older, already in college, and so our schedules had corresponded nicely. We were usually back in town around the same time. They were always hanging out, always up to something, even if it was just the two of them and a few other guys listening to old Radiohead albums and getting stoned from the makeshift gravity bong they'd set up in the bathtub. Andy texted back and said he was having people over, and I should come, and bring whoever along with me. He'd always had parties in high school and by eleventh grade he somehow managed to annex the entire third floor of his house; I don't think his parents have been up there since. It was always too dark in there—Andy went through this psychedelic phase and replaced the regular bulbs with ones that are tinted blue or red, which cast an eerie glow across the entire place. And it was always cluttered with books and old takeout containers, milk crates filled with old video games. Once I found an entire untouched pizza in a flattened cardboard box underneath the couch, coated with a thin layer of sickening green fuzz.

I wanted to go out that night, but I still felt slightly queasy at the thought of it, and before I left the house, I went to the bathroom and took a quick look at my ankle. The burn was healing; the blister had popped and now the skin was a little bit purple and wrinkled, but it was soft and painless when I touched it. I took out a book of matches from the mirrored cabinet and raised my leg up on the toilet seat. This time it was faster and easier; there was something almost mindless about it. I pressed the flame to my ankle in a different spot, closed my eyes, and counted to five.

❄

I felt surprisingly happy to be at Andy's house that night, in that warm, messy space. I sat down on the couch next to Josh and I leaned into the relief—the comfort of being with people who knew me well and yet not well enough to know how shitty these last couple of weeks had been for me.

"Josh," I said. "I miss you. How is everything?"

"I know! Pretty good, same shit. I'm going back up to Bard in a couple of days, right after New Year's."

"How's stuff going over there?" I asked.

"It's actually really good. I'm working with this really cool professor in the environmental studies department. We're working on this project to make the science building produce more energy than it consumes."

"That's kind of amazing." I said.

"Yeah it's pretty cool."

Someone passed Josh a joint. He took a hit and then handed it to me. "Be careful," he said, "it's so short, don't let it burn your fingers."

I inhaled, held my breath for a moment, let the weed infiltrate my body. For a little while I felt nice and relaxed, filled with an understated sort of elation. I felt just like the kind of girl who Daniel wanted me to be: cool and detached, happy.

A girl named Eliza walked in, someone I hadn't seen since the end of ninth grade. We'd gone to Hebrew school together years ago, when we were kids, and seeing her I immediately felt nostalgic, flushed with affection for her. I could picture us eight, ten years earlier, sitting in the synagogue cafeteria before class, drinking apple juice and stocking up on those cookies that were the kosher version of Oreos, the chocolate just a little less sweet than the real thing.

Eliza had always been pretty, but she had braces for many years and refused to smile, always kept her hands close to her mouth, doing her best to mask the clutter of ungainly metal laced across her teeth. But that night she looked poised and cheerful. Her father was Jamaican, and growing up she had this really striking, tightly wound curly hair that she hated. We'd spend hours at one of our houses, toying with blow dryers and straightening irons, a half dozen gels and creams, all promising that our hair would be straight and smooth, frizz-free. I thought about all that time we spent, trying so hard just to look like the people we wanted to be, and suddenly I realized how little I'd progressed since then. I still straightened my hair all the time, though now Eliza's was all natural—beautiful and curly, coiled and free, hanging just beneath her shoulders.

"Emma!" she said.

"Eliza! I was just thinking about you."

"I ran into your parents a few weeks ago, they were so sweet."

"Really?" I asked (and my whole body suddenly felt heavy, laden with worry at the thought of it—what had she seen?). "When? What were they doing?" I said.

"I don't know, maybe two or three weeks ago? It was just at the supermarket. I was so happy they even remembered me. We talked about the time they took us to that indoor amusement park upstate, in fifth grade. And how your parents squeezed into the kids' bumper cars with us."

"Oh my god, I haven't thought about that in so, so long."

"I know. I was actually so embarrassed, I don't know why I brought it up, but remember I got so carsick on the way back and threw up all over the backseat?"

"No," I said smiling, "what are you talking about?"

"Stop, I know you do. It was so gross. But your mom was so nice, I just remember I was crying so much and really worked up, and she came and sat next to me in the backseat for the rest of the trip."

I didn't remember this particular part of the story, but I did my best to conjure up the image, eager to see my mother the way Eliza did, maternal and kind, stroking her back so calmly, so benevolently.

※

JOSH hooked up his computer to this huge projection screen on the back wall, and a couple of minutes later we were watching a reel on YouTube of local news reporters with fluffy hair and business suits making egregious mistakes. One woman was saying "a top cock was injured in a car accident"; she kept trying to correct herself, saying "top cock, cock top," then finally she got it right, "top cop." Josh and Andy couldn't stop laughing. They replayed that one twice.

On the bottom of the screen there was a little ticker with the stocks going by and I thought, *What if there was a sign there for me, a coded message like the one my mother saw in those magazines?* Was

I supposed to be on the lookout for signals? And then I felt it, the familiar panic blooming inside me. What the fuck was wrong with me? My mouth was dry and my chest felt so fragile, as if somehow my heart could beat right through it and fracture my ribcage.

In the bathroom I sat down on a feathery teal-colored bath mat. It was slightly damp and littered with clipped facial hair. I brought my knees to my chest and rested my head against the soft denim of my pants. I called Daniel but he didn't pick up. I texted him: *I'm freaking out a little bit, can you please call me.* I tried to steady my breathing, but it was as if I could actually feel my brain refusing to let it happen. *I'm crazy. Crazy Crazy Crazy. This is really happening, I'm fucking gone.*

❋

AT home, after the panic had subsided and I felt a dreamy calm settling in, Daniel finally called me back.

"Hey sorry, I was at a movie."

"Why didn't you tell me?" I asked.

"Tell you what?"

"That you were going to a movie?"

"*Really?* Are we in that kind of relationship? It was two hours, come on."

"It's just that I'm kind of having a hard time, you know, and I would like to feel as though I could rely on you to like, be in touch."

There had been several of these conversations in the last two weeks and generally they went like this: Daniel would tell me that I wanted too much, expected too much of him, and I withdrew and was cold, and then, after a few hours in that uncomfortable, distant place, we'd drift back toward each other.

I wondered if later it would seem so obvious—how ill-equipped Daniel and I were to handle all this. Was it clear that I wanted something from him that he couldn't give me? Maybe I didn't even know precisely what that was—just something unconditional and all encompassing. But right then I hated him for not being able to take care of me, for not loving me enough to drop everything and be there when I needed him. For not wanting to hole up with me—to ignore everything else and just focus on soothing whatever kind of discomfort I was feeling.

"Can I change the subject for a minute?" Daniel asked that night on the phone. "I want to talk about New Year's."

One of his friends had rented out some "space" on the Lower East Side and was charging fifty dollars for an open bar, the whole night. I told Daniel I couldn't do that. I would barely want to go to something like that anyway, but it just felt too weird with my mother being in the hospital.

"But you went to a party tonight!" Daniel argued.

"It wasn't a *party*. It wasn't like anything was being celebrated, it was just a few people hanging out."

"Well, you don't need to *celebrate* New Year's. No one cares, it's not like a real celebration, obviously. It's just people having an excuse to get really drunk."

"Plus that's so much money, I would never buy fifty dollars' worth of alcohol. I just can't go to some big party on New Year's Eve and pretend that none of this is happening! I'm sorry if that's annoying, but I just can't."

"Well, I don't know what to tell you," Daniel said. "I get that this is hard for you, but your mom's not dying. She's gonna be okay. And I know it sucks that she's in the hospital, but *you* aren't, and you don't need to act like you are."

"Let me guess, you just want to be a seventeen-year-old dude and have normal, cry-free sex and get drunk and not have anything be a big deal?"

"That sounds like a trap, Emma, but yes, that's *exactly* what I want! What's wrong with that? I'm sorry that I just want to be a normal person and be happy and have fun on New Year's Eve."

I let out some sort of exasperated groan, ended the call, and threw my phone onto the carpet beside my bed. I just couldn't deal with him. But an instant later, my phone vibrated and there was a square of light in my otherwise pitch-black room. I leaned over to pick it up, assuming Daniel was texting to either apologize or admonish me. Instead, it was Phil. *Hey, you awake?*

chapter
10

I spent the next morning in bed, with my computer on my lap, re-reading old e-mails from my mother. They were ordinary in every possible way, except suddenly they felt like artifacts of a different time. In reality it was only a few months earlier that I'd told her about Daniel, and she'd responded,

> Like you said, I am "not going to make a big deal out of anything" but things with Daniel seem like they're going very well. Of course Daddy and I would love to meet him over Thanksgiving, but I'll leave that up to you . . .
>
> Your job at the dining hall sounds not quite up your alley (to say the least) but it's great that you'll have a little paycheck for yourself. You're working so hard, I know. Daddy and I are both very proud of you.

And just a month earlier, in the weeks between Thanksgiving and Christmas, she'd written,

Grandma fell today and I got a call from Saul early this morn-ing. She's okay, but will have to be in the hospital for a couple of days. It's unfortunate to have her so far away for the winter, but as I always say, it was her choice to move to Florida with her boyfriend. In any event, I'm sure she would love to hear from you.

I read through all of her e-mails from the past couple of months—once, twice, sometimes a third time. I was searching for some sign, some indication that this breakdown of hers was on its way. I tried so hard to find something ominous that I'd missed the first time around, but so far there was nothing.

※

A little while later I went into the kitchen—I could smell something cooking, maybe garlic or onions, and heard something sizzling. My father was dicing garlic and the counter was cluttered with glass bowls filled with finely chopped vegetables: red and yellow peppers, onions, thin spirals of orange zest. On the table he'd prepared a plate with scrambled eggs and rye toast with some jam. His back was to me as he worked.

"Whoa, look at this," I said. "What's going on?"

"I'm making some food to bring over to the Friedmans' tonight, so I thought I'd make you some breakfast too. Nothing special, just some eggs."

"Thanks." I sat down at the table, still dressed in what I'd slept in—a sweatshirt and some flannel pajama pants that my ninth grade boyfriend had given me. "What are you making?"

"Cellophane noodles and vegetables."

"What are cellophane noodles?"

"You know, those Chinese noodles, they're translucent and very fine. I used to make them all the time when you were a kid. With that peanut sauce you like?"

"You really need to do that right now?"

My father filled a pot with hot water and set it on the stove, added a sprinkle of salt.

"Need to? No. I just want to. What's the problem?"

"I don't know, it's just feels a little weird. Like, Mom's in the hospital and suddenly you're on steroids or something."

I felt shitty the instant I said it, as though I was some trope character, *the sassy daughter*, on a sitcom.

"You don't need to be nasty about it, Emma. I like being busy, productive. There's nothing wrong with that. Everyone deals with these things differently, I think you know that."

"Sorry. Thank you for making me breakfast." I scooped some forkfuls of egg onto my toast. "I guess I just wonder if it's the best thing. Like maybe you could just tell the Friedmans that Mom's in the hospital and you're having a hard time and you don't want to go, instead of making this nice fancy meal for them."

"It's not a meal, it's one dish. And I'd like to go."

"I guess, for me, it just feels a little weird doing normal things while she's trapped in that place, like a zombie, you know."

"I understand that sentiment, I really do, but I think it's important that we do try to do normal things," my father said. "You need to. Mom is going to be okay, she really is, and her recovery is not contingent on you staying home and keeping vigil for her. I've done that in the past, when you were younger, but it doesn't work, it's not helpful to anybody. And I think I've learned that this is the best way to handle things when your mother is sick."

"Okay," I said. "I get it, thanks."

But I didn't, not really. Unlike my father, this was all so new to me, and I couldn't help but feel the sting of those words, of my own ignorance. Having both Daniel and my father urge me to act like everything was fine didn't feel remotely helpful, and it made me feel so utterly lonely.

Daniel and I spent the rest of the afternoon arguing via different forms of communication. He texted to remind me that I went to his parents' Christmas party, so why was I protesting New Year's? I responded that I just wasn't feeling up to it, and that I wasn't mad at him and that I didn't care if he went to the party, I just didn't want to.

Then he called.

"I feel like you say that, and then I'm going to go out and then you're actually going to be really pissed."

"I'm not," I said. "I'm really not. Just enough already, please, I don't want to keep talking about this."

"You'll use this against me later," Daniel said. And he was probably right.

❄

PHIL was waiting for me outside my house just before five. It was one of those winter afternoons where the sky seemed to have turned dark impossibly fast. It looked as though it could've been the middle of the night. We were quiet, both of us, when I got into the car. We'd been thrown into a strange space—how do we act normally, casually, after exchanging so much intimate information, as we had just hours earlier over the phone? I stared out at the trees, all dotted with red and green light. And even though I really didn't like New Year's, couldn't stand all that pressure to be happy, I was dreading the end of the festive season. I'd come to rely on the way the holidays punctuated the days, broke up my time. There was something frightening in what January brought, that cold, dark, open space to just be there, be present.

The night before, I lay in my bed, on top of my comforter, the phone cradled at my shoulder, feeling nearly suffocated by the steady flow of heat from the radiator as I talked to Phil. I'd answered the phone drowsily when he called, but after a few minutes I was awake and alert, enlivened by the sweetness of his voice, the way he was so warmly forthcoming as he offered his story to me. He told me about his brother's second, most recent suicide attempt, though Ted's therapist had treated the first attempt as more of a *gesture*. This time was more definitive, Phil told me. I wanted to know, but didn't ask how he'd done it, and I'd imagined that Phil wanted to keep that part of the story for himself, press the weight of those small, particular details close to him, not wanting to send them out into the world.

"He's textbook bipolar," Phil said, "exactly what you hear about—waves of euphoria and then this horrible, crippling depression. I don't know how to explain what that's like, especially when Ted and I spent our whole childhood acting as though we were one person, when we share the same fucking DNA . . ." He trailed off and paused for a moment.

"The way I feel about Ted is like, how sometimes you hear pregnant women talk about their babies—you're 'thinking for two' now—that's how I felt, that he was always just this other part of my consciousness. And still, every time I feel super-excited or invigorated by something, I wonder, is this mania? Is that what it's like? But I keep having to remind myself that it's *his* disease, not mine. It's hard. It's a struggle. Especially when something like this happens, you know. I mean, then everything is different."

I envisioned Phil and Ted as two young boys sharing a small, cluttered bedroom: two twin beds side by side, identical dressers and piles of soiled clothing littering the floor beside them. Maybe a baseball bat or a worn leather mitt left carelessly in the middle of the room, and a fish tank in the corner, with a skeletal iguana crawling lazily from side to side, pressing his tiny, gummy fingers against the glass.

"In high school, there were times when I was so jealous of him and his mania," Phil said, interrupting the image I'd conjured of them as children. "I couldn't understand why he was given this incredible wealth of energy and creativity. He'd go through these periods where he never needed any sleep, and sometimes, in ninth and tenth grade, I would try my hardest to stay up with him, but eventually I'd end up falling asleep. I'd wake up a few hours later and Ted would still be awake, sitting at his computer, typing away furiously, writing a paper or working on some short story."

Phil kept talking for a long while, offering all his scattered, nuanced thoughts about his brother, compressed into this single monologue. I couldn't help but compare him to Daniel, who, only eighteen months younger, seemed infinitely less mature. Phil somehow came across as so wise—he was confident but humble, emotionally astute in a way that no other guy my age seemed to be.

It was after three in the morning when we finally got off the phone, and by then my eyes had completely adjusted to the darkness of my room. Everything had become visible—the words on the spines of the novels on my desk, the lacy straps of a tank top that hung from my chair, the frayed edges of a ribbon that Grandpa had been batting with his paws.

✳

THE next day, there we were in the car, just a few miles from the hospital. The trees were bare and white on either side of us, and they almost looked like ashy remnants of a forest fire. I felt an urge to take Phil's free hand, warm it up between my palms. He was underdressed in this icy weather, no puffy down jacket, no hat, just a zip-up fleece and a navy scarf tied loosely around his neck. And even something about his body struck me as more mature, more manly than Daniel's. His face had a sculpted quality to it, and his shoulders were broad, in a brawny, superhero sort of way.

"Are you excited for this wild night?" Phil asked me. "When was the last time you spent New Year's Eve in a locked ward?"

"Oh stop," I said. "It's not like that."

He smiled. "I know, I know."

"Though I guess, technically, literally, it *is* a locked ward."

"That it is."

"So what about afterward?" I asked.

"Afterward?"

"Yeah, I just don't know how long I want to stay there."

"Well, let's see, afterward we'll find a bar somewhere that hasn't acknowledged it's a holiday, and we'll go and talk about how much we miss the way our families used to be, and how going to visit them at the hospital is the *best* thing, the *only* thing to do, but how it breaks our hearts a little bit each time. We'll mope around a little, and then we'll get shit-faced? How does that sound?"

❋

PHIL and I walked upstairs where the hallway outside the dining room was busy with patients shuffling to get inside. The hospital staff was dressed entirely in black with cone-shaped, metallic gold-and-silver hats on their heads. They were handing out noise makers, glittery paper horns, and those festive gold-and-silver party hats to the patients, most of whom stared at them, bored and uninterested. Phil's brother, Ted, was sitting at a table with his roommate eating cheddar popcorn, their fingers covered in orange dust. I watched as Ted and Phil embraced—they slapped five—and did something between a hug and handshake.

There was an easiness between them that I admired. Each moment spent with my mother felt so intensely difficult, so hard to navigate. I barely knew how to talk to her; I analyzed each word both of us said, wondering if I'd uttered the wrong thing or if whatever came out of her mouth was some symptom of her illness. But that day it all seemed to matter a little less. I was there with my mother (we sat together and ate a bowl of seedless red grapes, talked about the activities that she'd participated in earlier that day) but I was focused on Phil, on whether or not he was aware of me from across the room, whether he liked the way my breasts pressed against the cotton of my T-shirt, or if he noticed when I took my hair down, let it hang just beneath my shoulders. I was lost in the subtle intricacies of our dynamic—was he looking over at me? When his hand had touched my back, fleetingly, on the way into the building, what had that meant?

And then there was a crash.

My mother had knocked over a pitcher of iced tea and it spilled everywhere, the ceramic shattering into a dozen pieces. She shrieked and a woman next to her let out a cry as liquid poured into her lap. Everyone looked over at us and I felt the heat of shame spreading across my face. Did they know that I had come to visit my mother but was not paying enough attention to her? Was focused instead on a guy—who was not my boyfriend—and the way he gracefully touched a kernel of orange popcorn to his lips?

"Oh Mom, I'm so sorry. I'm so sorry, are you okay?" I ran and got paper towels, helped the staff wipe up the table.

"I made a mess," she said softly. "Such a mess."

chapter
11

IT snowed while we were in the hospital and by the time we got outside, a fine layer of white was coating the pavement.

"Ever play the cold game?" Phil asked when we got inside the car. We didn't speak of the visit, didn't talk about how my mother seemed or how his brother was doing; we could've been pulling out of any parking lot anywhere. We granted each other that small gift.

"I haven't," I said. "Never heard of it."

All four windows opened simultaneously and a blast of cold air shot through; snow was drifting inside the car, bits of ice landed on my hair.

"Up! Up! Up!" I said. "Close up the windows!"

He grinned. "This is it," he shouted, "this is the game!"

"It's freezing!" I yelled. "Please!'"

We must've been driving fifty or sixty miles an hour. I pleaded with him to stop, but I was laughing too, swept up by all the noise and the cold, the snow rushing inside. I was gleeful and breathless.

My mind brushed free of the last hour. I felt like a tiny figurine on the inside of a snow globe, shaken into a flurry of white.

※

WE found a small dive bar off Route 28 with no bouncer, so we just walked right in. Inside it was dark and warm, and silver tinsel was sprinkled around the booths. There was a jukebox filled with pages and pages of CDs and a game console with two long plastic shotguns dangling on the sides. I put a dollar bill in the machine and picked two Linda Ronstadt songs, my mother's favorite.

Phil went to the bar and ordered me a whiskey soda. He had a fake ID that apparently always worked—a Connecticut driver's license that had belonged to a cousin who was just a few years older. I sat down in one of the booths and checked my phone. No texts from Daniel. One from Annie. One from my father wishing me a good night and saying he'd check in later.

"Phil," I said. "Can I call you Phillip? Does anyone call you that?"

"You'd be the first; it's actually Philo. Spanish. My mother's from Cuba."

"Ah! Explains your handsome, ethnically ambiguous look."

"Exactly," Phil said, smiling.

"How come I never see your family at the hospital with you?"

"Don't 'never' me. You've only seen me there once!"

I blushed, apologized.

"I'm kidding," he said. "And I don't know. My family visits, too.

But my parents work a lot and since I'm on vacation, I figured I might as well go a lot now, while I can."

"Maybe this is a stupid question," I said, "but are you angry at your brother?" Just then, "Hungry Heart" came on over the speakers. Hearing Springsteen right at that moment made me feel inexplicably happy. Something about the way he was both rugged and honest, earnest but without sentimentality. I drained my drink in one long sip, felt the whiskey tingle in the back of my throat.

"Look at you," Phil teased. "You love Bruce, huh?"

"I do!" I said. I was kneeling on the booth now, both elbows on the table.

"You asked if I was angry at Ted? No. So many people ask me that. But I'm not. I just don't see what there is to be angry about. He has an illness and is suffering. It's like, would you be mad at someone who had breast cancer? Of course not. And I *do* think that's a legitimate analogy."

"So I'm not supposed to be mad at my mother?" I asked.

"You're not 'supposed to be' anything. But are you?"

"I don't know. I guess I'm just mad at everyone," I said. I laughed, but realized it was mostly true. I twirled a flimsy red straw around the ice cubes in my glass. "I know that isn't fair but I guess I really do feel that way."

"I get that," Phil said, and took a sip of his beer.

"Can you get me another drink?" I asked.

"Whatever you say. Another whiskey?"

❋

WHEN Phil returned with my drink, I explained that everything with my mother had happened so fast. I hadn't even known she'd had any sort of history of mental illness, and suddenly it was all there: the voices, the paranoia, the hospitals. Everything so fresh and raw in front of me.

"It just makes me feel like such an idiot," I said. "And I feel so confused about who my mother is. Right now she seems like a totally different person than she was my entire life. I know it sounds dramatic but it's how I feel." I put my head on the table for a moment, and it was cool and sticky beneath my cheek.

"It's not dramatic," Phil said. "And I get that this is overwhelming for you right now, but it will change with time. This sounds like a cliché, but it's a cliché because it's true. Your mother has an illness, but that's it, she *has* it, it's not her whole identity. It's a part of her. Right now I'm sure it seems like all of her. But it's not, I promise."

I wanted him to know everything about my mother—what she had been like before all of this happened. I told him that even though she was a pianist, she also took two semesters of German in college and was somehow fluent, how she was so well read and always said she would've gotten a PhD in English literature if she hadn't been a musician. I told him that she was so thoughtful and caring, even if, yes, at times so overbearing that I would beg her, scream at her, to leave me alone. But when I was younger she was the mother everyone wanted to be around, the mother who always spoiled us with scoops of ice cream before dinner, who would make us vanilla milkshakes for breakfast if I had friends sleep over.

"She was that mom at sleepaway camp, wait . . . did you go to sleepaway camp?" I asked.

Phil shook his head no.

"Whatever, it's not important, just that like, at camp, getting mail was the most exciting thing ever, and packages! They were the best. And she would send these big boxes and all the kids in my bunk would rush over to my bed because they knew she sent the best candy—all that sour stuff, sour peaches and sour gummy worms, and then Pixy Stix and those balls of cookie dough covered in chocolate. Everyone would be like, you have the best mom, but of course, being my mother, it was obviously a little more complicated."

"How so?"

"Well, with the package, she would send floss and one of those little travel-size containers of mouthwash with a note reminding me to rinse and wash my mouth out after I ate. But then, there'd always be an envelope with my last few letters home, held together with a rubberband or something, with a Post-it attached, being like: *Hi sweetie. Daddy and I are so happy to hear that you're having a good time at camp! I circled some spelling mistakes and sent the letters back to you so you can see the correct spelling. Please remember, it's counse-lor. No A!* And all my letters would be like, edited with red marks and stuff."

"You're kidding."

"I'm not!"

❋

THE rest of the night passed quickly, but each of the moments felt so slow and drawn out. The bar never got too crowded. We took a couple of shots of whiskey and then Phil and I chose song after song on the jukebox, and we didn't quite dance but moved toward each other and apart, in a strange, awkward rhythm. I was drunk and sloppy. All of my longing—for Daniel or Phil, for my mother—felt like it was pouring out of me.

Later, Phil drove me home and I didn't even know if it was before or after midnight. My whole life my mother had always kept a single light on in the living room, which faced the street. That soft orange glow was meant to deter burglars and I had always been comforted by the thought of it, but then I wondered if this, too, was a symptom of her paranoia.

The house was dark, the driveway empty, and the street light cast a cold white light over the roof of the garage.

Phil turned off the car and I moved to face him.

"Please touch me," I said.

He put his hand on my leg, and I moved closer, touched the side of his face, felt the rough stubble of the beard that was growing in.

"I can't kiss you," I told him. And then he moved his hand gently across my face, my collar bone, then down to my breasts. I felt a shock of cold against my skin as he cupped my flesh in his hand. He kissed the skin above and below my nipple, so delicately. And he continued to move his hands around my body, into my pants, and then his fingers were inside of me and it did not quite feel good but I wanted it anyway.

"More," I said. *More, more.*

chapter
12

I woke up and started to move but then felt a wave of nausea sweep over my body. I thought to myself, *There is no way to undo what happened last night.* No matter how nuanced and complicated my relationship with Daniel might eventually become months, years from now, the simple fact that I cheated on him would always be there.

I threw up and then I got back into bed.

When I called Annie, she was careful not to judge me, and said something diplomatic like, "Well, it sounds like you felt like it was the right thing to do."

No, actually, I would not say it was the right thing to do, only that I wanted it.

Daniel hadn't texted or called, and I felt relieved. Maybe, just maybe, he hooked up with someone the night before and was feeling too guilty to contact me.

I spent the day alternating between self-loathing and apathy. I was the worst person in the world. I didn't care about anything at all. I took a lighter out of my underwear drawer and I burned a patch of skin on my calf until I could see the flesh bubbling up. And then I thought, *enough, enough.*

I went into the kitchen to get a glass of water and saw a note on the counter from my father that said, *At the soup kitchen. Tried to wake you but failed. Call me if you change your mind and would like to come. Dad*

I thought, *I hope that Phil never ever calls me again. I hope I'll never run into him at the hospital and that all of this will somehow disappear from my memory, from my history.*

I got back into bed, and I pressed my palms against my forehead, tried to alleviate the feeling that a stack of cinderblocks were resting there.

My grandmother called to wish me a happy New Year and to check in. She suggested I come out to Fort Lauderdale to visit, get out of New York for just a few days, maybe a long weekend. Her boyfriend, Saul, had a son-in-law who was a pilot and could get me free stand-by tickets. She said she would be here in a flash except that her hip was still a little bit too fragile from her fall, and she just couldn't travel at the moment. I told her I needed to think about it, but that the idea of a little trip sounded promising.

I watched an old episode of *Grey's Anatomy.* A teenage girl swallowed batteries, glue sticks, and a tiny stapler. Someone held an X-ray up to the light and the girl's insides were all exposed, the dark imprints in the space between her ribs and muscles.

The doorbell rang and I made my way to the front door slowly. My head throbbed with the slightest step. Ellen Friedman was at the door—the woman whose house my father had been to the night before. She said she was driving through the neighborhood and my father had left this nice glass dish at their house and so she thought she'd drop it off. She also brought over some leftover dessert from the dinner party. They were miniature pecan pies, each in their own foil container. "Oh thank you," I said, "that's sweet." She lingered for what felt like a moment too long, and then I had this sense that my father probably told her and her husband about what had happened with my mother. And here she was, just dropping by. I imagined that my father was infinitely more interesting to her now that something was dramatically wrong in our family—he was suddenly some kind of saint who was plagued by my mother's illness. I knew how it felt to fill with warmth, to love someone who was wounded (my ninth grade boyfriend's father was an alcoholic and at times abusive, and upon seeing the purple welts emerge on Ben's back, I would flood with sympathy and longing). I knew that strange place where the wish to care for someone and plain, romantic desire conflate. But then, at that moment, a primal urge to defend my mother kicked in, and it was as if I had guard dogs at my feet and they began barking at the first sign of an intruder. I would not let this neighbor think she needed to care for my father.

"My dad's not home," I told her, "but thanks, happy New Year," and then I closed the door.

I was in bed again and considered calling Daniel. I would tell him what happened and I would cry and plead and tell him how sorry I was and how messy and fucked up my brain felt. Would I tell him that Phil and I never even kissed? Would that make anything better? But I stopped myself; there was no chance he'd forgive me, especially after our arguments about New Year's, my refusal to go out and celebrate. He would think I was so pathetic, a sad, sad hypocrite.

When it got dark out, I started to check my phone compulsively and wondered if Phil would ever contact me.

The nausea returned, and I threw up again. I rinsed my mouth with horrible, minty, store-brand mouthwash and tried not to look at my ashen face in the bathroom mirror.

I held Grandpa in my hands. We were in my bed together and he was wrestling out of my arms but I wanted him to stay. "Please, stay. Please, please, please." I thought about what I must have sounded like, that desperation in my voice, and so I let go and he settled beside me on my pillow.

❋

THEN there was a text from Phil. He said happy New Year and asked how my day had been.

I felt relief undo some of the tightness in my chest and then immediately I called Daniel and asked him about his night, and I tried to just focus on the glow-in-the-dark stars that my father stuck onto my ceiling when I was a child. It had been years since they had emitted any light, and now all I could see was the faint outline of their shapes.

❋

MY father and I drove to the hospital the next afternoon. The air was windy and frigid and my father dropped me off at the entrance before parking the car. Upstairs, my mother was sitting at the edge of her bed with her knees pressed to her chest, her head bent down solemnly. She looked like a little girl who was waiting for her parents to check the closet for ghosts, or for monsters hiding beneath the bed.

Against the wall was a piece of purple construction paper. It said *CAROL* in large block lettering, and underneath it my mother had written: *caring, colorful, compassionate.* I felt a somewhat perverse desire to take out my cell phone and take a picture, to capture this image of my mother. She looked so wounded and afraid and I didn't want it all to myself. I wanted to show Annie or Daniel, my father, my aunt, anyone. As if sending a photograph out into the world could somehow disseminate my own heartbreak. Instead, I wrapped my arms around my mother, a gesture so affectionate (so unlike us), but I couldn't help myself.

"Mom," I said. "You okay? What's going on?"

She lifted her head and nodded toward the ceiling.

"What is it?"

"Nothing," she said, but it was barely audible.

I crouched down to meet her eyes.

"What's going on, Mom? What is it?"

"Just look!" She was suddenly screaming. She sounded so exasperated, so fed up, and my eyes immediately filled with tears.

"Please don't yell at me. What is it? What are you talking about? I don't know what you're trying to tell me." I wondered where my father was and why he was taking so long to get upstairs.

"The smoke detector," my mother's roommate said in her low, raspy voice. Debbie stood, erect, beside her dresser. Her hair was in a long, single braid, and she wore an oversized T-shirt with Gene Simmons's face emblazoned in the center. His tongue was long and reptilian, vulgar.

"Thanks, Debbie," I said. "What's going on with the smoke detector, Mom? What's wrong with it? Is it broken? Should I ask for a maintenance worker to come fix it?"

"No! No, no, no, no, no!" And then she was standing on top of the twin bed with her arms raised toward the ceiling.

"Please, please stop screaming! Just tell me what's wrong with it and get down, please."

"They are watching me from in there, Emma. There is a camera inside the smoke detector and people are monitoring me. They are watching. They can see *everything* that I do, so I need to take it down, okay? I need to take it down now!"

Two women in pink uniforms hurried in and they held on to her ankles, begged her to stop, to sit down.

"Ms. Bloom," one of them said, gently. "Please, hon, get down, please."

"I will not!" my mother said. "I. Need. To. Take. This. Off."

"What's going on?" My father appeared at the door. "What's the matter?"

"There is a *camera* inside of that smoke detector!" my mother yelled. "They think I'm a fool, these people. A camera right above my bed! Who can stand for that? I have some pride, you know!"

"Ms. Bloom, I promise you, there is no camera inside of there. It's just a standard smoke detector, maybe a carbon monoxide detector too. It's imperative that you leave that there, we need you to be safe in here."

"You call this violation of privacy safe? Safe?" My mother's voice rose each time she said it, and each time she spoke I felt something seizing, tightening inside of my chest. "Safe? This is safe?"

❄

I walked out of the room and down the hallway, searching for the bathroom, for somewhere else to go. I could still hear her screaming, *No, no, no, no, please no,* when I turned the corner and found it—a single room, tiled with black and turquoise squares. I turned on the faucet and I sat right down, cross-legged, onto the floor. I didn't care how filthy it may have been. I collapsed forward into my own lap and I wept. For my mother, for myself, for whatever I had done to make this happen.

❄

PAUL, the social worker assigned to work with my mother, was standing outside the bathroom speaking softly to another staff member. He was fiddling with the ID cards that hung from his neck on a long piece of yellow rope.

I wanted to tell him that my mother was not getting any better. I wanted to say, *What the fuck, what the fuck is happening here? It is your fucking job to help her. Why are you keeping her here, trapping her here, if you're not even doing anything to help her? Do you understand that nothing is getting better? That a month ago she was a normal person, she was my mother, who graduated eleventh in her high school class of nine hundred people, who was a prodigy pianist when she was a child, who played at Lincoln Center when she was seven! Who still strains orange juice for me because I'm the only one in our family who doesn't like pulp. Who, before I have a final, calls and asks me what time the test starts, so that she can worry for me, on my behalf, so I can just focus on studying.* I wanted to tell him that she was not just another crazy person in this crazy hospital, that she was *my* mother.

But instead, when he walked over to me, I asked him politely how long the medication usually took to start working, if he perhaps had a sense of when she'd really start to seem better?

"Unfortunately these things take time," Paul said. "We start seeing slight improvements, but generally it takes about six weeks for these things to really take full effect. If you want to talk to the psychiatrist, I can grab her for you. I'm really not the medication person. Dr. Kaplan can give you a better, more nuanced sense of what's going on with that."

"Okay, thanks," I said. "Maybe I'll talk to her some other time."

When I got back to the room a few minutes later, my mother had calmed down a bit, and the plastic shell of the smoke alarm hung limply from a wire. My parents and I decided to go upstairs to the terrace room. It was the third floor of the building that she was staying in—a wide open space with big windows and an angular glass roof. The late-afternoon light poured through the long dusty windows. The sky was changing colors, from pale purple to blue, and the horizon was low around us. It was beautiful but somehow grim, all those leafless trees, their bare branches waiting patiently for spring. There was a low-level chatter in the room, the muffled talk of the families who congregated uncomfortably at a series of round plastic tables: grown children visiting parents, a handful of couples who played board games tearfully. Sometimes it was difficult to tell who was visiting whom.

My mother still seemed a little shaken, a little weepy. I rested my hand on her back, on the pale pink cotton T-shirt slightly damp with sweat. "It's all right, Mom," I told her, "you're gonna be all right." She put her head down on the table and let out a little moan and my father walked away.

He stood by the window, with his hands buried in the front pockets of his jeans, a little bit hunched over. My father, quite literally, could never face his anger. He was generally so good-natured, so patient, but every now and then in moments full of tension, he just walked away, left the room, browsed a bookshelf, a spice rack, anything to avoid confronting an uncomfortable, painful truth. I was in ninth grade when my parents found out I'd been lying about sleeping at Annie's and was really at my boyfriend's, fooling around in the dank and dimly lit basement of his parents' house. I think this was when the idea of boarding school began to appeal to them—when they saw a flicker of some potentially dark trajectory, like maybe I'd turn into one of *those girls*. The kind who skipped class to smoke joints and sip forties in the parking lot, who carelessly let go of their virginities, propped up against a bathroom sink or in the backseat of an old sedan. Maybe I'd even get pregnant at sixteen and try to conceal my rounded belly beneath a loose-fitted sweatshirt, and just like that my whole life would veer off track. That night, they sat me down in the dining room and my mother said that we needed to start setting some serious limits, but my father had already wandered away, wandered into the den, where he probably stared blankly at the rows and rows of colorful CDs that lined his shelves.

"Do you want to play Scrabble?" my father asked when he returned. The table where we sat was stacked with board games: Apples to Apples, Trivial Pursuit, Scattergories.

"Okay," my mother said, softly. "Okay, maybe we should."

"We haven't played this in so long," I said. "Remember when I memorized all those Q words that had no U?"

"Of course, you'd walk around the house yelling out those words like you were practicing for a spelling bee," my father said. He unfolded the Scrabble board and we all picked out our letters. I got six vowels and a Z.

※

A woman with fiery red hair in a velvety bathrobe approached us, paused for a moment and then said, "I did a terrible thing, I swallowed the sperm of a man who was not my husband." She went to every table and said this, like a waitress reporting the daily special. When she came back to us a second time, my mother grabbed her hand and said, "Marie, it's okay. It's okay, sweetie."

Even there, despite her madness, she offered that warmth, showed that instinct to be generous with her love. And there in the terrace room I saw the briefest, slightly heartbreaking, flicker of her old self.

chapter
13

IT was snowing heavily, two days later, when I met Daniel's mother for lunch. If my mother had been around, she would've insisted that I stay home, that the drive to the station wouldn't be safe, that the roads would be slick with ice and sleet, and that even the train itself was more dangerous on days like this. I went anyway because I needed to keep busy, keep moving.

I had somehow been able to convince myself that nothing had happened with Phil, that our flirtatious texts were only that, and that everything was normal with Daniel. But every so often I felt seized by guilt, a hollowing out of my insides, an ache in a place I couldn't quite name.

On the Metro-North train into the city, I took my shoes off and sat cross-legged on the vinyl seat. My coat rested like a blanket across my chest. I got lost in a dark fantasy about my mother where she never got any better. She went from hospital to hospital and eventually my father decided to move her into a group home—some big Victorian house where she shared a bedroom, ate meals, and partook in communal activities with two dozen other adults who could not care for themselves. I saw her name on a laminated chore wheel stuck to the refrigerator. Some days she would sweep or clean the bathrooms. Other days she would stand in the kitchen and skin potatoes and carrots, like some sort of forlorn zombie with an apron tied loosely around her waist, muttering to herself about the malevolent spirits trying to hurt her through the heating vents. I imagined that my father would have a girlfriend—someone smart enough and kind enough, but she would have none of my mother's depth. She would be too skinny and do lots of yoga and drink smoothies and she would not have any sense of irony at all. She would say stupid things like how great it was that we lived in a post-racial society and that I needed to accept, or even embrace, my mother's illness to really know and love her true self. I wanted to pour a steaming cup of coffee straight into the lap of my father's imaginary girlfriend, onto her white linen pants.

I started crying somewhere in the Bronx and the sweetly sympathetic ticket collector stopped and asked if I was okay. He looked so young, like he could've been fifteen, with one of those faint mustaches growing in, just some downy hair above his lip. He had a hole-puncher in his hand and he clicked it absently and then stuck some tickets into his breast pocket.

"You okay?" he asked. "Need a tissue?"

"Sorry, thanks," I said. "I'm okay, just some family stuff."

"Oh," he said. "Been there."

As I said the words *family stuff*, it felt like a lie even though I knew it was true. A kind of shorthand for any number of things, but it was marked with a particular significance, as if it gave me license to wallow, to fuck up and act out. And now that was exactly what I'd done—used my *family stuff* to get drunk and sloppy with Phil. It felt so cheap, like it was just an excuse to be an asshole with flimsy morals. What felt the worst was that my family had always been so uncomplicated (not that it had been perfect—there were years that were punctuated with lots of unpleasant yelling and the fierce slamming of doors), but now things felt different, truly fractured. I had always felt this kind of smug superiority when people complained about their families—parents who'd had an ugly divorce and were using their kids against them, or had an estranged brother or uncle whom they hadn't spoken to in a decade. But I saw then that none of us was impervious to this kind of tangled, familial mess. We were never *really* in the clear.

※

I met Daniel's mother at EJ's Café on Columbus and 84th Street and I was covered in sleet by the time I got there, my hair crunchy with ice. There were only a handful of other people in the restaurant— an elderly couple sitting beside each other and sharing a tuna fish sandwich, a pair of red-headed children across the booth from their father, sipping chocolate milk out of two oversized glasses.

Jane ordered coffee and a beet salad; I got a grilled cheese sandwich on rye bread. I'd been feeling so on edge and was in this constant vaguely nauseated state. All I wanted to eat was simple, bland food.

For a while Jane and I talked about other things, the classes I'd signed up for next semester, Daniel's sister's travels. It wasn't until the check arrived that Jane asked about my mother, how she was feeling, how we were both doing.

"It's like there's simultaneously both too much and nothing to say," I told her.

"What do you mean?"

"Every day it feels like so much is going on, but I spend time with her at the hospital and nothing is actually happening. I don't feel like she's getting any better."

"It takes time," Jane said. "Do you know what she was taking before all this happened?"

"No! That's the thing. I knew and know nothing. Maybe she was on something and stopped taking it? I have no idea."

"That's very common," Jane assured me. "People take their medications and they work so well that they feel like they don't need them anymore. It happens all the time. Or sometimes they don't even stop taking them but the meds need to be readjusted, a little more of this or less of that. But I think you can trust that your mother will return to her baseline; it's just a matter of time."

I told her about my panic attacks. That they came out of nowhere and made me feel like I was losing my mind, that my heart just sped up and I couldn't seem to align myself with reality, to the actual moment that I was in. That I had these moments where I was terrified I was going crazy.

"Emma," she said, and something in her voice was both stern and calming. "Your mother has an illness, but *you* don't. Having anxiety is actually a *healthy* reaction to what's going on right now. You're going through a lot, but I promise, absolutely promise, that you'll be all right."

I wanted to tell her about the information I'd read—that the average onset of schizophrenia was twenty-five, so I was definitely not in the clear, not yet. That she couldn't know for sure that I didn't have it. That according to the research I'd done, if you had one parent with schizophrenia, there was a 10 to 15 percent chance that you would develop it as well. And so, at that very moment, schizophrenia could've been there, lying dormant in my brain, waiting for the precise moment to strike. But I wanted to believe Jane, I wanted to let her comfort me and felt so relieved that she had answered with such certainty, that suddenly I was so hungry. I finished my sandwich, dragged some remaining fries into a puddle of ketchup and stuffed them in my mouth.

"Have you ever done yoga? Or any kind of mindfulness, breathing exercises?" Jane asked.

"No, I'm bad at that sort of stuff. It's okay, I'm okay."

She offered to refer me to a therapist she knew, someone *brilliant*, she said, who could really sit down and talk with me, *unpack all this stuff.*

I thanked her and said I'd think about it. I drained the rest of my coffee, which was now chilly and sweet, the sugar all resting there at the bottom of the ceramic mug like grainy cement.

❄

WE stepped outside and though it had stopped snowing, the air still felt frigid, impossibly cold.

"I would love to take you somewhere nice," Jane said, wrapping a long orange scarf around her neck. "I never got you a Hanukkah present. Maybe we can make a quick stop at Bloomingdales?"

"No, Jane! That's ridiculous, so unnecessary."

"It would be a real treat for me. My daughter's been gone for months so I haven't been able to take anyone shopping! Maybe we can get you a nice new hat? Or a bag? That tote you're carrying is ripping at the seams."

We stopped at the corner and waited for the light. There were discarded Christmas trees everywhere. People had been depositing them on street corners, leaning them against garbage cans. The side-walks were littered with pine needles, and when I looked down for a moment, the pavement, ornamented with so much green, could have been mistaken for the floor of a forest.

❄

DANIEL and I fell back into our old routine so effortlessly and I felt relief sweep over me. I couldn't undo it, but as more time passed I could convince myself nothing had really happened with Phil, and it felt like I was driving farther and farther away from the scene of a crime.

All the news outlets warned that a big nor'easter was coming and we had to prepare for the worst: buy food, fill bathtubs with water, stock up on batteries and flashlights. Jane went to the supermarket and came back with bags and bags filled with groceries.

"All stocked up!" she said

Daniel and I helped put the food away. There was arugula, fresh mozzarella, eggplant, baby carrots, a bright orange block of cheddar, a block of Parmesan, three different kinds of breads (a French baguette, a loaf of whole wheat, some pita pockets), a roasted chicken, and some deli meats too, smoked turkey, slices of prosciutto.

Just before five, Daniel and I decided to smoke a joint and go to the planetarium, which was only a few blocks from his apartment. We were about to walk out the door when Daniel said he forgot something. He brought back a little sock puppet with googly eyes and gray yarn for hair.

"What *is* that?" I asked.

"You don't know who this is?"

"Einstein? Your grandpa? I don't know!"

"It's Sir Isaac Newton."

"Stop," I said. "You're so cute. When did you make this?"

"It's not cute, it's manly. He should come with us, he loves astronomy."

As we walked over to the museum, we held hands and Daniel

told me facts about Isaac Newton: he was born tiny and premature and nobody thought he would survive, he was raised by his grandmother, he was brilliant but was also considered a tyrant. *And*, he suffered two nervous breakdowns during his lifetime.

Every so often Daniel surprised me with this erudite side of his and I felt like such an idiot for ever doubting his intelligence.

❋

AT the planetarium, we sat in the back, in plush velvet seats, and looked up at the fake, majestic sky. We were still in our puffy coats and snow boots. I whispered to him, "Do you remember that episode of Friends where Ross and Rachel come here?" Daniel smiled, kept looking straight ahead.

"Don't ruin this by comparing us to Ross and Rachel," he said. "But look up, there's Orion." He pointed to the cluster of lights above us.

There was something about this wide open sky that felt so safe and comforting. I had never known what to think or feel about God. I always said I was an atheist but I crossed my fingers behind my back as I proclaimed it. But that night, beneath the beautiful, artificial sky, I felt protected by an invisible force. Like the whole world was one enormous womb, and I felt some maternal god stroking her belly affectionately. I said this out loud and Daniel laughed at me.

"My little stoned philosopher," he said and he rubbed his palm against my stomach.

"I love you," I said. "I really, really do."

The walk back to Daniel's house was only four blocks along Central Park West. We were still feeling high and happy and I imagined that the moment we walked back into the apartment, we'd be shuttled back into another reality.

We stopped and sat down on the stoop of a building next to Daniel's. On the corner, a man stood beside a small cart, shielded from the wind by the long orange flaps of an umbrella. The smell of almonds and peanuts dipped into hot cinnamon and sugar was sweet and potent in the air. I leaned toward Daniel and put both my hands into the fleece-lined pockets of his parka. I told him that I might have to go to Florida for a couple of days to visit my grandmother, that I was just feeling so disconnected from my family and maybe it would be nice to get away for a while.

"That will be good for you," he said, and I wasn't quite sure what to make of those words, but I tried not to read into them too much.

❄

THERE were half a dozen pairs of shoes in a pile outside the door of the apartment: a pair of men's loafers, Daniel's charcoal-colored Pumas that he'd had since eighth grade, a pair of pumps and equestrian-style riding boots, and some navy blue orthotics that must've belonged to Daniel's grandmother. There was something about the sight of that messy pile of shoes that made me want to cry—that ordinary evidence of familial life. I held Daniel's hand and kissed the scratchy fabric of his jacket, pressed my mouth against the sleeve.

Inside his bedroom, Daniel removed his clothes and did a little striptease, theatrically taking off his clothes for me. He unzipped his fly, flung off his belt in a dramatic gesture; next was his T-shirt, which he twirled around with his index finger.

"Stop it," I said. "You're too cute."

He pushed me down onto the comforter.

"If you ever call me cute again," he warned. I wrapped my legs around his naked body, pulled him toward me, pressed my face into the warm hollow of his neck.

❅

THE next morning we woke up and discovered that the forecast was right; the sky looked as though it was fuming—it was snowing and hailing and flakes were flying sideways across the windows. Across the street, Central Park was cloaked in white, no one was walking their dogs, no doormen lingered beneath awnings. It was quiet and motionless.

All transportation was shut down for at least a day: MTA, Metro-North, LIRR, and New Jersey Transit. It was a relief to be trapped here, with Daniel and his family, a relief to have nowhere else to go.

"So much for global warming," Daniel's grandmother Nora said. She was small but not frail, and at eighty-nine, she still lived alone in an apartment a few blocks west. She read the *New York Times* every day and could crack walnuts open with her bare fists. (*Don't you ever try to mess with her*, Daniel had warned me the first time I met her.)

"It's called climate *change*, Ma," Daniel's father said. "*Change* doesn't mean it's always getting hotter."

We sat around the living room and played Taboo. Nora said we all talked too quickly but it turned out she was the sharpest player, her guesses so swift and astute.

A bowl of pistachio nuts sat on the coffee table and I took a handful, tried to crack the shells open into my lap. Daniel took the tough ones and pried them open with his teeth, lovingly spitting the meat into my palms.

"Sweet," I said. "So sweet."

I wanted to be part of this family. And I felt flooded with guilt and gratitude and sometimes I couldn't quite distinguish between them. But within minutes, in the middle of a round of Taboo, while Jane was laughing, frantically trying to convey the meaning of some secret word, I was seized by panic. I stared at the purple and green Taboo cards that had been discarded onto the rug, each with a list of words on them, and I thought, *Is there some message here for me?* My mouth went dry, and all I could feel was this nagging, incessant feeling that something was terribly wrong in my brain. My body felt empty, like my muscles and bones—everything that kept me solid and together—were gone. It was just my heart, thudding frantically, bouncing around my insides like a marble inside a pinball machine.

I tried to make eye contact with Jane after her turn was over. She sat with the dog perched on her lap and curled the white fur around her manicured fingers. If I were losing my mind, she would know, wouldn't she? She was trained to look out for these things—to detect people's mental instability when they weren't sure of it themselves.

"I'm feeling kind of nauseous," I said, abruptly. "I think I'll go lie down for a little bit."

I went into Daniel's room and I lay down on top of his red comforter—it was soft and worn, from his childhood, the reversible kind that was crimson on one side, royal blue on the other—and I tried to steady my breathing, control my thoughts, but my heart wouldn't slow. I felt certain that this feeling would never, ever go away. That I'd have to go to the hospital, and if I crossed that line, could I ever come back? Maybe I would need to go back out there and tell Jane I was freaking out. *I'm losing my mind, you have to help me.* I imagined myself in the closest ER, bleak and dirty, with bright fluorescent lights. In my mind it was more like an interrogation room. Maybe I would even end up at the same inpatient facility as my mother. *Mother-daughter hospital suites.*

I tried to slow my breathing Lamaze-style, like I'd seen so many times on television. I relaxed my diaphragm. I stared at the decorated walls; the blown up cover of a Wilco album—pale yellow background and huge, looming circular towers in downtown Chicago; an old collection of Absolut ads from the nineties that Daniel had pasted onto one corner of his room; and that iconic Rolling Stone cover of a naked John Lennon in a fetal position clinging to Yoko, his arms wrapped snugly around her head. That was what I wanted right then—to hold on to Daniel, to find the deepest sort of comfort in his presence.

I kept waiting for him to come in, to come see if I was okay. I took his iPod out from the dock on his night table, and I scrolled through the album titles, trying to distract myself. I found a playlist called *For Nina* (Nina was a girl that Daniel dated before me, for most of his sophomore year) and if it had been any other time, I probably wouldn't have looked, but I wanted to feel that particular prick of jealousy, a tangible pang, anything other than that raw, unrelenting panic. I imagined Daniel combing through his thousands of songs, carefully picking out the tracks to impress Nina, to convey feelings that maybe he otherwise wouldn't have been able to. A lot of them felt mostly benign (some Talking Heads) or just really blatant (Bob Dylan's "Mama, You Been on My Mind") and then I got to that Tom Waits song, "I Hope That I Don't Fall in Love with You," and I stopped, had had enough. My panic had momentarily abated and was replaced by anger. Every minute that passed that Daniel didn't come in to check on me left me feeling more heated and lonely. I tried to sleep. I brought my knees up to my chest. I counted slowly backward from one hundred like my father taught me to do when I was a child.

Finally he came in and I kept my eyes closed and he touched the tips of his fingers against my cheeks to see if I had been crying.

"You don't even care!" I was sobbing.

"I'm trying Emma, I am! What do you want me to do? Am I supposed to know what you're thinking every minute?"

"I don't know! But what are you going to do if I actually start to lose my mind? Not everything is just easy all the time, and if you actually love me like you claimed to last week, you would give a shit!"

I had an urge to peel off my socks, show him my bare ankles, my slightly wilted flesh on display for him. *Do you see? Do you see how much I'm freaking out?* But I didn't, I just cried and I held on to him and I thought about how much I needed him, how clear it was that he didn't love me enough, not nearly as much as I wanted him to.

"I'm trying," he said again, quietly. "I really am."

Our bodies found each other and sex gave us that momentary respite, a diminishment of our problems for just that little while.

✳

LATER that night, I was still feeling that slightly intoxicating relief that followed in the wake of panic. We went downstairs to the apartment of Daniel's friend Maggie, someone he'd known since childhood. She'd gone to a prep school in the city like Daniel but by eighth grade she'd developed a coke problem and had subsequently gone to half a dozen boarding schools. She had finally ended up at one of those reform-type schools in Utah, where I imagined teachers threw you out into the wilderness alone, asked you to defend yourself in the woods for days, with only a compass and a bag of trail mix. Maggie was beautiful and so confident in a way that I'd never understand. I was sure that she and Daniel had hooked up at some point but I just couldn't bring myself to ask because I didn't really want to know.

"I don't think Maggie likes me," I told Daniel while we were waiting for the elevator.

"You always say that when *you're* the one who doesn't like somebody."

"Shut up!" I punched him gently in the shoulder. "Sorry. I love you."

He didn't say anything.

"I said, I love you-uh."

"I know-uh. Look, Maggie's just one of those people who gets along better with guys."

I groaned. "I hate that. I hate girls who hate girls."

"Blah blah blah. You hate everything."

"Not true! That is sooo not true. I love my friends. And playing Taboo with your family. And my family. And reading. And getting high and going to the planetarium with you."

We stepped into the elevator—all mahogany and brass—and for a moment I lifted up my T-shirt and my bra, exposing my chest for Daniel to see.

"Emma!"

"Daniel!"

"Put those away," he said. "There are cameras in here, you little show-off. Those are for me to see and no one else."

I felt a pang of shame, and then something warmer inside my gut as I thought of Phil—his cold fingers, the feel of his facial hair against my mouth.

❋

DOWNSTAIRS, Maggie was sitting at the kitchen table rolling a blunt (that was so the kind of thing she would do, not smoke a joint, but a *blunt*).

"Hey guys," she said, "how's it going?" Her voice was low, raspy. A guy was sitting next to her who I assumed was her boyfriend, with long dreads twisted up into a bun. He stared at his phone and barely looked up when we got there.

✳

"MY parents aren't coming back for a while," Maggie said, "so we can do whatever. Feel free to take a drink from the liquor cabinet."

"Let's go to the carousel," her boyfriend suggested.

"Sure," Maggie said. "But we have to be careful." We filled glasses with vodka and Diet Coke and walked down the hall. Daniel whispered to me that Maggie's stepdad collected carousel horses.

"I'm sorry, what?" I asked.

I followed them down the hallway, and into an otherwise empty den.

The horses were beautiful. Half a dozen wooden ones, mounted on posts, and like a carousel stopped in time, each horse was at a different height, their legs bent midair. Maggie gave Daniel her drink to hold and swung a leg over a glossy saddle.

"I mean, it's ridiculous," she said. "So embarrassing. But whatever. I love them. They're my babies."

"This is amazing," I said.

Maggie brushed her hand along a fake mane—so polished and smooth. I stared at the horses' eyes, wide and watery. There was something so sad, so human about them.

I had an urge to text Phil. For some reason I assumed that he would appreciate the absurdity of this moment. *I'm at an apartment that literally has a carousel in it*, I typed. But then I copied and pasted it into a text for Annie instead. She wrote back immediately. *What does that even mean? Miss you.*

※

AFTERWARD, I told Daniel that I thought it was so annoying when white kids had dreads.

"How do you know he's white?" Daniel asked.

"I mean, he obviously is."

"Maybe he's not. Sometimes you're so judgmental."

I sat with it. I was judgmental. He was right, he just was.

"But admit it's still annoying," I said.

"What's annoying about it?" (Phil, I found myself thinking, would totally get why this was annoying.)

"It's like appropriating someone else's culture," I explained.

"You wear those little suede shoes with the beads on them."

"Moccasins? That's not the same thing." But then I wondered if it was, if maybe Daniel was right.

※

I LAY in bed beside Daniel, but I couldn't sleep. I made a mental list of all the things that were wrong between us. And no matter how excited and swept up I had been at times, if I was paying close enough attention, there had always been something off—a tiny wire that hung loose, leaving us the slightest bit disconnected. I'd always worried that he thought I was too dark, too analytical, constantly picking at things. *I'm sorry that I don't, like, get the human condition,* he'd told me once, when I'd been complaining about this nagging feeling of emptiness, some longing that I didn't quite know how to fill. But since my mother had gotten sick, this was something that had begun to plague me even more; I couldn't be this effortlessly cool, carefree girl that I wanted to be for him. I was angry about the time he picked me up at the hospital with Jamie in the car. And I was still angry about that night at school when he told me he had a migraine and was going to sleep early but really did shrooms with his friends. Sometimes I did this thing where I imagined him talking about me to his next girlfriend. *She had a lot of problems, she just, like, wasn't a happy person. She was so critical, always complaining.* I didn't want to be whatever I thought Daniel thought I was—that flawed, unhappy person. I crawled over and pressed my lips to his neck, which was so warm, always, as he slept. *Baby*, I whispered. But he was sleeping, or at least pretending to.

※

THE storm had come and gone impossibly fast. The next morning was sunny, the temperature in the forties. Yesterday's clean stretches of snow were already gray and dirtied, etched with footprints. I wanted to understand how everything could change so quickly. How my feelings could ambush me. How my mother could be so fucked up, so gone. How I could love Daniel, feel sick with guilt, and then suddenly, desperately, want Phil.

chapter
14

I had been back in Westchester for a day when Phil texted and asked if I wanted to go to the hospital with him now that the bad weather had subsided. But I couldn't. Or maybe I just didn't want to. My last visit had left me feeling both anxious and suffocated, and the last thing I wanted was for Phil to witness my mother have a meltdown. Or perhaps equally as bad, for him to see me, the way I panicked, as I watched my mother have a meltdown.

Instead, we decided to get coffee the next day, to meet at a little café halfway between our houses. It was the type of place with exposed brick walls and Christmas lights and big leafy plants that hung from the ceiling.

"I hate coffee," Phil said, smiling, when we walked inside.

"Oh great," I said. "Glad we came here then."

"Will you pick something else for me to drink?"

He sat down at the table and I ordered him an Earl Grey and poured in lots of honey. It was one of those plastic bottles shaped liked a bear, and I squeezed its belly, pinched the plastic flesh together. I noticed that Phil's beard was growing in. All of his features were so dark, but the tiny hairs that came in beneath his cheekbones, above his lips, had a reddish glow to them. That he had a beard seemed like some symbol of his manliness. I tried to control the impulse to compare Daniel and Phil, but it was difficult. Daniel's face was so smooth, and at times I loved to brush my lips against its surface, but there was also something so enticing about Phil's scruffiness. Suggestive of some acquired wisdom.

We picked at a cranberry scone together.

"I hope you're not upset about what happened the other night," he said.

The other night had felt so long ago already, like so much had transpired between now and then.

"I know you have a boyfriend and everything," he said, "but I just want you to know that it's okay. We were just a little drunk and we're both going through a hard time and that's all."

"Yeah, I agree. It's all right," I said, and then I mumbled something about trying to be friends, if we could. But my nonchalance was feigned in both directions—I somehow felt simultaneously queasy with guilt, but also intensely, crazily attracted to him. I wished that things weren't so complicated. I didn't want him to say it was okay, to blame it on our drunkenness; I wanted him to want to rescue me from my perfectly good boyfriend, who loved me, who was more than adequate but somehow still wasn't enough. And I wondered why I always wanted more, why I wasn't ever really satisfied.

Phil's phone was face down on the table. It buzzed next to a slim, bent paperback copy of William Styron's *Darkness Visible*.

"Is it good?" I asked him. I hadn't read the memoir, but I knew about Styron's crippling depression.

"I'm not sure. I always do this when my brother's having a hard time," Phil said, "try to just immerse myself in whatever other people have to say about it, if that makes any sense."

I told him it did, but that for me, right then, I felt exactly the opposite—I'd barely been able to read, or to focus on anything at all, for more than a few minutes.

Phil's phone kept vibrating and he flipped it over for a moment, dragged his finger across the screen and groaned.

"It's my brother's girlfriend," he said. "Or whatever she is. She keeps texting me. She always wants to come to the hospital to see Ted and I don't know what to tell her. She's stressing me out."

"Well, what does your brother think?"

"He doesn't really care at the moment. They're hardly dating now anyway. They've been in this on-and-off-again thing forever, and I guess they're sort of off right now. Or they were, but then this happened and she just popped in. She's kind of a melodramatic mess. The kind of person where everything always becomes about her."

"It's a weird thing," I said, "how when somebody is sick, you start to feel really territorial about them. Like you start to feel the need to prove your love, your loyalty."

"You think I'm doing that?" he asked, and he picked at the corners of the scone.

"Well, it sounds like your brother's girlfriend is doing it a little bit, no? Maybe we all do to a certain extent. Or I do, I know I do. I feel this pressure to prove that I love my mom more than my dad does. And I know it's bullshit, in a way, but I really do feel it, this urgency to show that love."

At the table next to us, a baby was screaming. Her mother gently rolled the stroller back and forth, while the older sister sat on her knees picking at a black-and-white cookie, skimming the frosting off the top with her tiny fingernails. We made eye contact for a moment and then she got up, climbed off her chair and faced me.

"Do you have Fruit Ninja on your phone?" she asked.

I laughed. "Unfortunately I don't."

"That's okay. Do you have Scramble?"

"I actually don't have that either. I have Boggle, though."

"That's not the same."

"Sweetie, leave her alone, please," the girl's mother said. I smiled at her, told her it was all right.

"If I give you a dollar, will you buy an app for me?"

"How old are you?" I asked.

"Six and three-quarters, how old are *you*?"

Phil seemed oblivious to this little creature beside me or maybe he just didn't care. "Somebody once told me that having a mental illness turns you into a narcissist," he said. Hearing that, the little girl gave Phil an exasperated look and went back to her seat. "And in a way it turns *everybody* into a narcissist. Even when it's about the other person's affliction, everything becomes an issue. It's like this hyperawareness and heightened sensitivity, all the time."

"I know what you mean, it's like we all just isolate ourselves further and further," I said, "spending so much time in our heads, analyzing whatever happened, and grieving alone."

"Well," Phil said, "at least we're not really doing that." And there was something in his voice that I couldn't quite figure out. Maybe he was flirting with me, or maybe it was just the simplest kind of relief, a respite from loneliness.

I told Phil that one of the biggest problems I was having right then was my habit of continually questioning everything, going over things in my mind, incidents that had happened with my mother years and years ago, looking at everything through this lens of her illness.

"Like after you have a really bad breakup and then you go back and undermine your entire relationship, wondering if it all ever really happened?" Phil asked.

"Yes, exactly."

I told him about the time in seventh grade when, for women's history month, I'd planned to do an oral presentation on Stevie Nicks. I'd read my mother some of the facts I was planning to tell my classmates, among them that the cartilage in Stevie Nicks's nose had atrophied because of all her cocaine use. My mother was horrified, and an hour later had provided me with a list of female authors for me to consider instead of Stevie Nicks. There were probably others, but the ones I remembered were Virginia Woolf, Sylvia Plath, and Anne

Sexton. And now, in retrospect, it seemed impossible to ignore what bound those three together.

"I see what you're saying," he said. "Things become tainted."

"Exactly."

"But it's complicated. Those women were all such talented writers, maybe your mother just loved their work. And also, all those women were depressed. Your mother isn't, right?"

I shook my head. "No, she's not, I mean I didn't think she was, but obviously I don't have the best judgment in regard to her mental health, so who knows."

I rested my hands around the ceramic mug of coffee and for a moment he leaned over and touched my face.

"You're so cold," he said.

✳

AFTERWARD, we lingered in the parking lot. I stared down at the gravel and made a square in the dirt with my right foot. I felt him looking at me and then felt my face flushing.

"What!" I said, smiling. "What are you looking at me like that for?"

"I know we aren't allowed to do anything," he said, "but can we just hang out again? Just a little? Really, just to talk and do whatever?"

He grasped me playfully, and I wondered if he was going to kiss me or hug me but then he just rubbed his knuckles into the mess of my hair, a sloppy bun that rested on the top of my head.

"Maybe a little," I said and I twisted myself out from his grip, did a clumsy twirl. "Maybe we can hang a little."

❋

THERE was something about being with Phil that made me feel so at peace with myself, like in that very moment things weren't such a fucking mess, as if my thoughts were actually linear and rational. But the instant I got into my car, I felt the weight of everything—my guilt, my self-doubt, my anxiety. It was as if I were driving on the highway during a bad storm, and then just for a moment I was beneath an underpass and everything was suddenly normal— the weather was calm, the rain gone. But within seconds I'd driven through the underpass, and water was slapping across the windshield again, loud and unrelenting.

❋

AFTER the conversation with Phil about his brother's girlfriend, I started to wonder about my parents; what had it been like when my mother had her first psychotic break all those years ago? Why had my father stayed with her, and was he ever plagued by his decision? It seemed almost impossible to imagine—they were barely older than I was and had been forced to deal with really serious issues (it wasn't as though my mother had some chronic sinus infection that my father would be aware of every so often).

It occurred to me that I knew so little about my parents' relationship, particularly about that time in their lives. All I'd seen were a handful of artifacts: dried lilies from their wedding pressed into a cellophane sheath; an old Tufts spiral notebook of my mother's, in which she had doodled my father's name in small, tightly wound script all over the back cover (this had been kept for decades, in the attic of my grandmother's house in Queens); a photograph of my parents from their junior year that was paper-clipped to a program of a recital that she was in. She was dressed in a short paisley dress and her hair was straight—apparently she'd ironed it on an actual ironing board—parted down the center; my father was in perfectly round wire-rimmed glasses and sporting something resembling an afro.

I parked the car outside my parents' house and put the heat way up and let it idle, which I knew my father would've yelled at me about. I thought of my mother's friend Andrea, whom I imagined had been present for so much in my mother's life—my parents' courtship, her first breakdown, who knew what else. But I didn't have her number and instead texted my aunt Elaine.

Are you busy, can we talk?

I have a million questions for you.

I waited for her to respond and turned the car on and off every few minutes, waited for the cold to seep back in and then put the heat back on. Elaine called a little while later and I said, "Can you just tell me everything about that time? From when my mother first got sick and went to the hospital? And what had my father been like then?"

She exhaled heavily. "Oh sweetheart, it was all so long ago."

"I know," I said. "I know, but just whatever you can give me."

"Well, I was still in high school," Elaine said. "I was a senior, and was about to go off to George Washington in the fall, but your grandmother really babied me and so in a lot of ways, even though I was eighteen, I was so young, so naive, really. We got this call from your father, it was the spring, probably early April? And he just said that he was concerned, that your mom hadn't been acting like herself. I actually remember that I was sitting in the living room with my friend Laurel, and—this is a horrible story—she died the next summer, in this horrible freak accident at a summer camp, where she was a counselor. She and another counselor were sailing in one of those tiny little boats out on Lake George, and it just capsized."

This was the sort of thing that my mother had done all the time while telling stories, veer off topic, talking about a million different things. It had always annoyed me but I found solace in it in that moment—this thread that connected my mother and her sister. I let my aunt continue for a while, let the conversation wind its way back to my parents.

"How long had they been together by then?" I asked. "Did you and Grandma already know him well?"

"Well, he'd come here for Thanksgiving, so we'd already met him several times. We were already really fond of him . . . I don't remember the specifics, but he and your mother had been together for a year or two by then?"

"Okay, sorry, continue," I said. I turned the car off again and I saw my next-door neighbor bent over on his knees sorting through his recycling. I stared at the band of exposed flesh peeking out below his waistline.

"Look, it was terrifying," Elaine said, getting my full attention. "But I don't remember all that much. Your grandmother and I went up to school. It was springtime and the campus was so beautiful— everything in full bloom, lots of kids all over the quads, smoking grass, protesting this thing or that. It just felt like the most exciting place in the world to me. And then we get to your mother and she looked so sick—I'll never forget this hollow look in her eyes. She was my big sister, you know, and she was just . . ." Her voice trailed off.

"Gone?" I asked, thinking of my mother in the hospital that first day, how distant she had seemed, how far away.

"Yes," Elaine said. "She was gone."

We were quiet.

"Are you still there?" I asked her.

"Your mother," Elaine continued, "was wearing layers and layers of clothing, that image I'll never forget, pajama pants over corduroy bell bottoms, and then this blanket wrapped around her waist. She looked terrified. As though putting on all that clothing could some-how protect her from whatever it was that was torturing her. I don't know . . ."

"And what about my dad? Where was he throughout all this?"

"He was just so good to her. He's a natural caretaker, he always has been. When bad things happen, he steps up. He took charge, but not in a domineering sort of way, not at all. You know, our father had died all those years ago; we hadn't had a man in our lives in so long, and so he just kind of naturally assumed the role of the man in our family."

"Right." I wondered why this hadn't occurred to me before. It seemed so obvious.

"I don't know that much about your father's parents, to be honest," Elaine said. "But I do know that they were conservative and not totally pleased with him—they wanted him to be a doctor or a lawyer, a banker, whatever, and he was too much of a bleeding heart for them. And your Grandma Ruth and I, we just loved him. We welcomed him into our family. We'd been wanting a man in our lives for so long, and there he was."

I imagined then that my paternal grandparents must have resented my mother, must have wanted, as all parents did, a normal life for their son, and there he was, twenty-two years old with this difficult burden that had fallen so heavily upon his shoulders. Did everyone think my father was some saintly martyr who gave up the gift of a normal life for this troubled woman he loved? I had begun feeling so territorial about my mother. I didn't want my parents' whole marriage, our whole life together as a family, reduced to this single, unhappy narrative. It made me sick but I couldn't think of it any other way.

"Emma, I'm so sorry, but I have to go," Elaine told me. "Uncle Jack and I are going into the city to have dinner with some friends and he's waiting for me. Can we talk later? Tomorrow?"

She and Jack had some tiny terrier that they dressed up in argyle sweater vests, and I could hear his high-pitched barking in the background, begging for my aunt's attention.

"Yes, of course, of course," I said.

"Look, the whole thing was awful. It was a nightmare. But she got better, she just did."

I got out of the car and walked slowly around the neighborhood. I saw swimming pools that were covered by charcoal-colored tarps that were littered with twigs and leaves, lit-up living room windows, televisions broadcasting the six o'clock news. I walked forward and back, pressed my feet against the overgrown roots of a tree I used to climb as a child. It was freezing cold but I was sweating beneath my down jacket and I kept unzipping it every so often, needing to feel the cold air against my exposed skin.

I thought then that I understood why my parents had been so reluctant to discuss the details of this unhappily complicated part of their past. It was simply too hard for them to say the words out loud. It was like families who just couldn't bear to walk into the bedroom of a deceased child or sibling. The rug on the floor, the bedspread, the posters on the walls, all of it left untouched for years. How hard it would be just to open that door. The rush of grief that would spill out from the tiniest crack.

chapter
15

I was on the plane to Florida, struggling to get my bag up top, and I felt myself beginning to sweat, felt the pressure of the string of passengers who were waiting behind me. A man across the aisle held a bag from Taco Bell, the paper damp with grease. The smell, something sour and peppery, made me queasy. But then a stewardess came over and in one graceful motion lifted my suitcase into the air, packed it neatly into the overhead compartment.

Once I settled, breathing in the stale air, the faint smell of antiseptic, I started to relax, to sink into the comfort of flying. There was something about that literal suspension, about being held in the air for three-and-a-half hours, that I found so liberating; there was nothing to do but read or listen to music, no one to report to, nothing expected of me.

I picked up *Anna Karenina*; I was still only a couple hundred pages in, couldn't seem to get any further. I kept getting distracted, and now I was drifting into thought, replaying scenes from the night before in my head. My father and I had gone to dinner at a kitschy Chinese restaurant in White Plains. (I tried to think of all the times we'd gone out together without my mother, but all I could think of was when we saw *Finding Nemo* at a big multiplex on the Upper West Side and when I took him to see Neil Young at the Meadowlands for Father's Day last year.) The Chinese restaurant was elaborately decorated—the exterior was tiled with those faux Asian-styled roofs and ornamented with clusters of red paper lanterns. We shared chicken with cashews and an order of vegetable dumplings, a big pot of tea. Our interactions felt stilted, as if some kind of sticky web had grown between us. I asked what would happen when he went back to school this week, who would visit my mother while he was busy and I was in Florida? "It's just a few days," he said, pausing with his chopsticks midair, a piece of dark-meat chicken caught between them. "I'll go after work one of those nights. Aunt Elaine will visit too. Don't worry so much."

I stared at a nearly empty bowl of white rice, picked up each remaining grain with my fingers. The fortune cookie was stale, and it had crumbled into my hand when I tried to open it. On the way home from dinner, Phil had texted me, *Can I come see you before you leave?*

I called Daniel, promised myself that if he picked up I wouldn't see Phil. But Daniel didn't answer, and I texted Phil back right away. *Yes*, I wrote. *Just for a little.* And that was when I returned to that mental list, all the things that were wrong between Daniel and me—so I could justify my longing for Phil.

When I got home after dinner, I didn't even bother going into the bathroom or closing my bedroom door. I took a lighter out of my bag, rolled up my jeans, pressed the flame to my calf and counted to ten. There. It was over and done with. All my feelings swept up in one simple gesture.

Phil came over shortly after my father went to sleep. We sat on my bed and talked. He made fun of all the things in my room that rooted me so plainly in adolescence; the magazine cutouts pasted on my walls, the old ottoman made out of inflated plastic (this had once been such a fad), photographs of Annie and my cousin Molly tucked into the corners of my bulletin board. But then he kissed me and what followed all seemed to happen inexplicably fast. He was on top of me and moving and his mouth was so close to my ear, I could feel the heat and moisture of his breath against my skin. "Are you coming, are you coming?" he asked.

But I didn't answer, couldn't explain to him how that wasn't what this was about, not tonight, and I just held his sweaty hair in my hands, pulled him closer to me. He moaned as he came, let out a cry so sharp it seemed he might almost be in pain. I pressed my hands against his back, my legs still wrapped around him. "Stay," I said as I could feel him starting to pull out. "Don't go, not yet."

We lay in bed and I told him about the conversation I'd had with my aunt, how it made me admire my father in certain ways, but how

I also resented the idea of him as some sort of hero or martyr who had given up so much to be with my mother.

"Maybe it's less complicated than that," Phil said.

"How so?"

"Maybe he was just really in love with her, despite her illness, and wanted to be with her."

"You're such a little romantic," I said, and I planted a kiss sweetly beside his temple (an oddly intimate gesture, I realized afterward, and I moved one of my legs so that it was no longer intertwined with his).

"I'm serious! I mean, it just seems like a pretty un-nuanced view of their relationship."

"It is, of course it is, that's what made me frustrated, seeing it in this one-dimensional way. My mother has contributed so much to their marriage, obviously. She's the backbone of our family in so many ways."

"Right, so just make sure you keep seeing all that stuff, the full picture," he said.

"You mean stop fixating on little things—stop obsessing over the idea that my father's parents probably think that he ruined his life by marrying some young, crazy girl?"

"Ha, yes, precisely."

Grandpa had been sitting silently, coiled up like a snail, beneath my desk chair. He leapt up onto the bed and nestled himself right in the space between our heads. Phil reached out and brushed the fur beneath his neck. I loved watching him do this, felt oddly moved at the simple, tender gesture.

"But even if your grandparents did see it that way, so what?" Phil said. "Your parents have been married for what, like twenty-five years? They obviously grew to know her as more than that."

"You're right."

"I know this isn't the same thing," he said, "at all, but my mother is really adamant that I marry someone Catholic. And she just doesn't understand how hard it is to meet *anyone* you like at all, let alone enough to marry. And it's like, if you're lucky enough to find someone you love that much—"

"Exactly!"

"Then even if they're not Catholic, or if they end up going crazy . . ."

He rolled over and faced me and I brushed my hand over his prickly facial hair.

"Oh, so you mean, you want to marry me even though I'm Jewish and I might be genetically inclined to have a nervous breakdown soon?"

I was kidding, obviously, but part of me wanted to tell him how frightened I was of becoming my mother, of losing my grip on reality, slipping into dangerous delusions, feeling paranoid and completely overcome by some kind of malignant spirit. But I worried that admitting this fear was only further evidence that it could easily happen to me, that maybe it already *was* happening to me. I wanted to know how much Phil feared turning into his brother—they shared an identical genetic makeup. How could he not be terrified?

He traced his fingers along my stomach and then down my thigh.

I wondered if he would see the three burns on my legs, and if he would say anything. There was a part of me that wanted to tell him about this, the only relief I could find. Did he ever feel so overcome with guilt about his brother's suffering that harming himself seemed like such an obvious, easy way to even the score? But I didn't want him to know, not really, didn't want Phil *or* Daniel to see how much I'd been unraveling. How unhinged I felt. Though it felt obvious that if anyone would get it, it would have been Phil.

"Oh yeah," he said then. "I'd stay with you forever and ever, even once you lost it. Even if you were shuffling around in a Seroquel-induced haze, with those little paper slippers they give you . . ."

"Okay, okay, enough!" I slapped him lightly. The conversation had taken a dangerously loving tone, and I knew it was mostly a joke but I felt uncomfortable nonetheless.

I had only slept with two other people before Phil, and the fact that we had somehow stumbled into this *thing*, whatever it was, made me feel simultaneously so sophisticated but mostly incredibly young, ill-suited for juggling two relationships when really I could barely handle one.

Before he left, Phil put an old issue of the *New Yorker* on top of my dresser, next to all the bottles of nail polish and dusty candles. He told me to read the Jonathan Franzen essay about David Foster Wallace, about what it was like to love someone so sick, how difficult and complicated their friendship was.

On the plane, I opened up the magazine, read more about Wallace's battle with mental illness, his subsequent suicide. Phil had underlined this one paragraph: *How easy and natural love is if you are well! And how gruesomely difficult—what a philosophically daunting contraption of self-interest and self-delusion love appears to be—if you are not!*

I kept thinking about that line, but I didn't know who was well and who was not. It felt so easy to love, *that* I could not control, but so hard to know what to do with that love, so hard to love *well*. I rested my head against the tiny oval window, and I stared out at the fields, the mazes of swampy greenery, thousands of feet beneath me.

chapter
16

IT had been nearly a decade since I'd been to Florida, but the moment I walked out of the airport and felt the rush of humid air, I was flooded with memories. I thought of the time in second grade when my family and my cousin Molly drove down from New York. The whole trip was about ten days, and I missed two days of school. (Two days I *always* regretted missing, when the eggs our class was watching over finally hatched and cracked open, and those twiggy, fragile chicks sprang to life. By the time I returned to school, they were already full and round, chirping loudly and on their way back to the farm.) I remembered the long stretches of driving through the south, and finally when Molly and I saw the sign welcoming us to Florida, bright blue and ornamented with oranges, we ripped off our sweatshirts, as though the crossing of a state line indicated a sudden, severe change in weather, and the two of us screamed with sheer excitement. And then, a few years later in fifth grade, we went to Universal Studios, and I got sick from eating too many of those hot dogs wrapped in pretzel dough and threw up all over the fake New York City sidewalk.

My grandmother, Ruth, and her boyfriend, Saul, were waiting for me in a long white Buick, which looked like a relic of a different era. Ruth was small and round, with bands of flesh around her waist. She was wearing a yellow blouse and linen pants. Her hair was cut into a little bob, dyed reddish blond. She was seventy-eight and had always looked so young, but her hip was still slightly damaged from her fall in November, and she was using a cane to prop herself up, standing beside the car. I was startled at the sight of it.

"Emmala!" she cried, and we embraced warmly. She examined my face and then hugged me, repeated that motion a couple of times. It had only been a few months since we'd seen each other, but I imagined she was feeling particularly sad and nostalgic, having just recently moved down to Florida year-round, anticipating what it would be like to go months without a visit from family.

Saul stepped out of the car, walked around from the passenger side, and gave me a quick hug, then took the suitcase from me. He was wearing clean, white, thick-soled sneakers and a pair of salmon-colored shorts.

"How was your flight, honey?" My grandmother asked.

I climbed into the back seat of the Buick and I told them that it was mostly fine, that there had been a girl sitting behind me on the plane who gave herself a full manicure and pedicure. I could hear the sharp, metallic sound of the clippers, smell the acetone of the polish remover.

"I didn't say anything, obviously," I continued, "but some guy sitting across from the girl freaked out and there was this big fight."

"That's the kind of thing people get killed over if they're not careful," Saul said.

❋

SAUL and my grandmother lived about fifteen miles south of Fort Lauderdale, in a small city by the water, with wide open streets dotted with palm trees, lots of elderly Jewish women, and a handful of their remaining husbands. There were clusters of apartment complexes—tall white buildings and glass patios, gleaming turquoise pools. It was warm and balmy, the sky always some sweet pastel, the color of sherbet.

❋

MY grandmother had had an apartment there for a dozen years, since she retired as an elementary school teacher in the late nineties. She was living there seasonally, shuttling back and forth between this apartment and her house in Queens. It wasn't until she moved down there that she met Saul. She'd been single for almost forty years by then, my grandfather having died in his late thirties, following a heart attack in the middle of the small men's shoe store he owned on Ocean Avenue in Brooklyn.

Ruth was a single parent from then on, teaching extra classes during the school year and in the summers too, to support her children. And everyone in our family was a bit stunned, when, after so many years of solitude, she brazenly announced that she'd fallen in love. It was just a few months ago that she'd sold her house, and she and Saul moved in together in Florida.

"We are so, so thrilled to have you visit," she told me now. "My friends can't wait to meet you."

❋

SO many things from my grandmother's house in Queens had been transplanted into this apartment. A bowl, in the center of the table, filled with papier-mâché fruits and vegetables: an eggplant, a tomato, a pair of oranges. A wall of photographs recreated in precisely the same arrangement as it had been in Queens: portraits of grandchildren, some pictures from a trip we'd all taken together to Club Med ten years ago—my cousin Molly snorkeling, surrounded by white trees of coral. One of me as a toddler in long footie pajamas, asleep and slung over my mother's shoulder.

There was the bathroom drawer filled, just like it used to be, with old makeup. Waxy tubes of pink lipstick, plastic compartments of blush, complimentary samples of perfume in tiny bottles that clanked together like wind chimes when I sorted through them.

❋

THE three of us went out to dinner a short drive from their apartment. It was a seafood restaurant with a giant lobster that hung menacingly over a red roof. My grandmother and I shared a broiled salmon, our favorite kind of fish. She and Saul asked me about school, about Daniel. Saul readjusted his hearing aid every so often; when I spoke, he leaned toward me so he could hear better. We didn't talk about my mother. Or we did, but not about what was happening then, only the past.

Saul told a story about his twin granddaughters, who had just recently come to visit him—without their parents—around Christmastime. They were seven, and one became so homesick that she literally made herself sick, he said.

"There are so many fun things to do, we went to the beach, to play miniature golf, but no matter what it was, she cried. By the time she left, she could barely speak, her voice was so hoarse from all that crying!"

"Oh, I used to have such bad separation anxiety from my mother," I said. "I'd cry hysterically even when she was only going to the supermarket."

"She did," my grandmother said, turning to Saul. "Sometimes when she was at my house without her parents, she'd miss her mother so much. Hours would pass and finally, when I knew that Carol would be coming back soon, I'd let her go wait by the door. She was always trying to look out of the small oval pane of glass in the center. But Emma was such a tiny little girl, and so I had to bring her a small stepladder. And she would stand on it, her head peeking out above the glass, just enough to see a slit into the outside world as she waited for her mother."

She reached across the table to touch my hand.

"Oh my poor Emmala," she said. "It was the sweetest, saddest sight."

❋

IN the parking lot, my grandmother and Saul held hands as they walked slowly, purposefully, toward the car. Saul's hands had grown puffy, swollen with age, I imagined, and they had a paw-like quality to them. I had wondered if all those years alone had hardened my grandmother in some way, but there was a gentleness between her and Saul, and I was surprised to see how sweet they were together, how delicately they embraced one another.

❋

I had decided I wouldn't talk to Phil while I was in Florida, and so I kept turning my phone off or deliberately leaving it at the apartment. When I got back after dinner that night, there was a message from Daniel. I had hoped and imagined this trip would be enlightening in many ways, that I could just clear my head and focus on myself and my family. But even in Florida I couldn't stop analyzing things with Daniel and obsessing about Phil.

I imagined going to visit him at school; I saw us aimlessly roaming his leafy college campus, drinking beers at a noisy house party and then curling up in a tiny twin bed together. I thought about kissing him, casually, just turning my face toward his whenever I felt like it. And each time I got too caught up in the fantasy, I made myself sit for a minute and think of my mother. I thought about that night at the A&P, the faraway look in her eyes, the way the yellow light from Best Buy illuminated her blank face. I tried to conjure up the terror in the pit of my stomach, the sensation that I was in some sort of horror movie and my mother's body had been invaded, taken over by a zombie.

The words were slippery inside my head as I sat in my grandmother's guest bedroom, but I tried to grab hold of them: "schizophrenia," "mental hospital," "my mother." I spent a few minutes just focusing on the images, the phrases. And then the drama with Phil and Daniel seemed to subside, just the tiniest bit.

I took the elevator downstairs and called Daniel back. There were a couple of overhead lights on, casting a bright yellow glow over the pool. I sat on the steps, in the shallow end, and rested my feet in the warm, heavily chlorinated water.

Daniel told me that he wanted to figure out when we were going to head back to school, and that his friend Tom wanted a ride back with us, too. I just really hadn't been thinking about school at all— I'd been so consumed by everything going on, the idea of leaving seemed almost implausible.

"Well, you're gonna have to go back eventually," Daniel said.

"Yeah, obviously."

We were silent for a moment.

"What are you doing tonight?" he asked distractedly, as if we were both in New York, and he was making plans for us for the evening.

What do you think I'm doing?

"It's nine o'clock," I said. "I think my night's pretty much done. And look," I told him, "you should go back to school whenever you want to. I'll probably end up staying a little longer than you. Maybe I'll take a bus or train back."

"Are you sure?" he asked.

"Yes, totally."

Recently, I'd begun trying to imagine what Daniel thought about our relationship. Could he sense that something was wrong? Every so often we were perfectly aligned and then other times he and I seemed to be looking at two totally different relationships. Or perhaps it was just as simple as our moods not matching up with each other; I could never quite be sure.

＊

I heard my grandmother and Saul up early the next morning—their muffled voices, the cautious opening and closing of cabinets. I stayed in bed until eight-thirty or so and then went out onto the patio where they were eating breakfast. I'd caught them mid-conversation, their words peppered with Yiddish, my grandmother emptying a packet of Sweet'N Low onto a rosy grapefruit half.

I had this immediate though vague memory from my childhood, walking into my grandmother's kitchen in Queens. She was eating rye bread and jam, holding a cup of what was probably instant coffee. She was with her sister and they were mostly speaking in Yiddish, but I also heard them cursing, my grandmother saying *shit*, repeating it again, *shit, shit, shit*.

Suddenly I found myself wondering if this was when my mother had been hospitalized all those years ago. Would I even have been able to remember this? I knew absolutely nothing about that time, none of the details. What season was it? What month? How long had she been in the hospital for?

My grandmother offered me some fruit as I sat down in a plastic lawn chair. A little glass table with ornate wrought iron legs held a bowl of sliced melons, a pot of coffee, a plate of toasted English muffins.

"Do you want me to make you something?" Saul asked. "Some French toast? Or we might still have some frozen waffles left over from when the twins were here."

"This looks perfect," I said, and I helped myself to some cantaloupe.

※

AFTERWARD, I changed into my bathing suit—a multicolored string bikini that I hadn't worn in months. It was stretched out and the cups a bit too small, showing too much of my skin, the side of my breasts a little too exposed. My skin was so pale, shrouded in sweaters and jeans and winter jackets all season. Downstairs, lying out by the pool, I could see my body plainly for the first time in months, out in the light, in the sun. The bruised, rippled circles of blistered skin along my ankles, two spots on my calf. I'd felt so strongly, only three weeks earlier, that I'd needed this marker, this gruesome evidence of my painful, conflicted feelings toward my mother, but suddenly, looking at those scars in the bright, clean light of morning, I wanted them erased. I wanted my unmarked skin back, unmarked save for two scars—one dulled line from an appendectomy, another tiny scar on my right cheek, from a dog bite I got in fourth grade after a neighbor's terrier sunk his teeth into me.

I had quite literally branded myself, I thought, and pulled a towel up over my legs.

❊

SAUL was in good shape for eighty-two. He swam laps every morning and I watched as his fleshy arms sliced evenly through the pool. My grandmother had the *Miami Herald* unfolded in her lap, along with a pair of big plastic knitting needles and some lavender-colored yarn. I was browsing the latest issue of *People* that I'd bought the day before at the airport, was happy to be so easily sucked into its brief, provocative stories: a Kardashian was pregnant, a Teen Mom was filing for divorce, a burly, orange-colored cat somehow found his way from Michigan to Ohio.

A few of my grandmother's neighbors joined us by the pool. They were warm, effusive women in their late seventies or early eighties. They were all in remarkable shape: their minds sharp and agile, untouched by disease or senility. They told me how much they loved my grandmother and Saul. One, in a bathing cap ornamented with plastic daisies, told me that my grandmother was the "most wonderful" addition to their book club, that she offered "the most insightful comments."

"And Saul," she continued, "well, we're all lucky to have him, what a handy man he is to have around. And a good driver, too. Plus he can still drive in the dark!"

"They're just using me for my boyfriend," my grandmother joked.

※

MY grandmother and I drove to a mall in Fort Lauderdale that felt more like some sprawling, tropical compound than a place to shop. Lots of terra cotta buildings connected to one another; palm trees lined the paths between them. Living in Florida brought out a side of my grandmother that wasn't apparent in Queens; she indulged herself just a little bit more. Where in New York she would save tinfoil, reuse Saran Wrap (her old depression-era habits), here she would get a manicure, allow herself to order a scoop of sorbet and a glass of wine along with her main course.

At the mall, we went into stores like H&M and Urban Outfitters, but my grandmother couldn't understand how people could pay lots of money for things that were deliberately meant to look cheap. She kept pointing at loose threads and faded denim, see-through cotton T-shirts. I chose the most respectable, conventional crew-neck sweater I could find from the Gap so that my grandmother would think her money was well spent.

At the food court, we settled on frozen yogurt; she got a vanilla with no toppings, and I ordered peanut butter chocolate chip with little pieces of Heath Bar crumbled on top. We hadn't talked about my mother once all day, and I could feel it coming on, as if we were on a date and finally needed to discuss what our status was.

Within moments I heard her say, "We need to talk about your mother, Emma."

"I knew it!"

"Well, it's important," she said, burying her spoon in the yogurt. "It's a lot for a young person like you to deal with. And I want you to know that it's okay for you to be angry—if you are—with anyone, with all of us. Your mother, your father, with me, that we didn't tell you sooner. I think we were all just hoping she would stay in remission forever."

I liked the word "remission"; its sharpness, its official, medical feel. I said it in my head. *Remission.* I wanted to be able to hold onto it, preserve it. Return to it later when I needed to.

I thanked my grandmother and told her I didn't know if I was angry or not; the feeling came and went.

"I always thought you should know your mother's history," she said, "but it was their decision, I was up front about that."

A couple sat down next to us. They were deaf and signing to each other. I stared at their hands, their gestures graceful and fleeting.

"Your father tells me you've been very, very attentive to your mother," my grandmother said pointedly, getting my attention. "I know she appreciates that a lot. You're a good daughter, Emmala, you're wonderful, you really are."

I could feel my eyes start to well up.

"I just wish someone could tell me what's going to happen," I said, suddenly overcome, exasperated. I didn't know how to articulate this, how I wondered, every day, if my mother would ever return to her old self, if our relationship would ever be the same.

"When your mother first got sick, in college," my grandmother said, "I had this terrible, terrible fear that nothing would ever be the same. That I had lost her, forever. But no, not so. It comes and goes. Our relationship has changed, we adapt, we move along with her illness. Does that make sense?"

"I think so."

"If you want to know, will she still be the mother who nags you to brush your teeth, will she make sure you clean the shower with one of those squeegees so that the glass doesn't sprout mildew, will she call you when you're thirty years old because it's freezing outside and she wants to make sure you'll wear a scarf? Yes. I think all those things. When she is well again, she will."

※

WE were out by the pool again the following morning. Saul was dutifully swimming his laps while my grandmother and I sat on plastic beach chairs, united by a striped yellow umbrella shielding us from the sun. My grandmother held the Arts section of the *Times* propped up in front of her. "I like to see what I'm missing out on up there," she said, smiling.

I took out my paperback of *Anna Karenina*. A romance was stirring between Kitty and Levin, and I was picking up speed just a little but still struggling in some way to connect with the narrative. I was never quite in it, always conscious of how many pages I'd read, how *productive* I was being.

"Can I take a look?" my grandmother asked. She reached for the paperback, held the hefty weight of it in her hands. "I loved this book so much," she said.

"Really? I'm having some trouble getting into it."

"God, I read this about a hundred years ago, twice, actually. Once, when I was in my thirties, a few months after your grandfather died. The other time I was a child, really, twelve or thirteen, maybe. I read it to my grandmother."

"You read her the entire book?"

"Yes, she'd gone blind so early. This probably wouldn't have happened today, but by the time she was fifty, she'd completely lost her vision. And she was such a good, devoted reader, she wanted to read all the time. So after school I'd come home and read to her. You can imagine how long *Anna Karenina* took," she said, "but I wanted to. I loved my grandmother so much and she took such pleasure from it." She leafed through the book, somewhat wistfully, it seemed, as though those hundreds of pages somehow contained her past too. And maybe, in a way, they did.

"This was almost sixty-five years ago," she said. "Oh god, I feel so old even saying that!"

I imagined little Ruth in her dimly lit tenement on the Lower

East Side. A one bedroom shared by the entire family, which then consisted of her mother and grandmother, and her baby sister, Harriet. I saw my great-great-grandmother's long white hair pulled severely into a bun, her broad pale face, thick black glasses. I imagined chicken soup and chopped liver and I wondered if this bore any resemblance at all to what my grandmother's childhood was actually like. I thought of how envious I'd been of Daniel's family, how much I'd romanticized their affection, but suddenly I felt firmly anchored by those women, my ancestors, so rooted to our history, which felt both invisible and enduring.

MY grandmother and Saul had a little barbeque on the patio and invited their friends over for dinner. My grandmother and I sliced up watermelon and pineapple while Saul worked on the grill. It was a cool night; the sky was a cloudless pale indigo. Their neighbors arrived with some wine coolers. They asked me about boarding school, told me about their book club—their current selection was *Madame Bovary*. They talked about a particularly raucous tennis match that had taken place earlier that day. Saul passed a plate of grilled portobello mushrooms to my grandmother and gingerly kissed the top of her head as he walked by. These were not the people of old age homes, I thought. They seemed so content, so at peace, their lives still full and textured.

I wanted to tell them how lucky they all were. That my mother, thirty years their junior, was sitting in a hospital, eating her meals in a dining hall surrounded by dozens of people who stared emptily at one another, making jewelry with uncooked pasta, painting their feelings with watercolors.

Saul made a little toast, to having me there with them. "To Ruth and her family," he said, "which now includes all of us." My grandmother started to cry. She was such a rare combination—a paragon of strength who cried at the slightest gesture of kindness. I put my arm around her, took a sip of her peach-flavored wine cooler.

IT was my last night in Florida and I couldn't sleep. I was in the guest room, stretched out on a sofa bed with soft floral sheets, staring at the small boxy television on top of the dresser. I watched reruns of *Friends*. They were back-to-back, two hours of episodes so far.

Beside the bed were a handful of framed photographs of my aunt and my mother from their childhood. In one, my mother, a teenager, wore a yellow dress, the skirt long and pleated. She and her date stood outside my grandmother's home in Queens, posing beside a long crimson Oldsmobile. In tiny condensed script someone had written, *Carol and Richie, Senior Prom.*

My mother was smiling in a slightly embarrassed, knowing way, and I imagined her begging my grandmother to stop taking pictures, to let them leave already. Just a few years after that photograph was taken, everything in my mother's life would be radically different. I felt a kind of terror mixed with heartbreak, thinking about the dramatic irony—looking at those photographs, how innocent and naive she appeared, but knowing how cruelly her mind would betray her.

Years from now, would somebody see a picture of Daniel and me outside of our dorms, lying leisurely on the campus quad, and feel the same thing about me? How many years left of sanity could I count on?

I realized I hadn't had a panic attack once in the three days I'd been in Florida. I wanted to believe that meant something, was indicative of my mental health, but there was no way to be sure. When I was a kid, maybe nine or ten, I had a stomach virus and was up all night in the bathroom, my mother holding a cool washcloth to my forehead, rubbing my back as I retched, over and over into the toilet bowl. I'd asked her how much time would have to pass before she knew I was okay, before I wouldn't be sick anymore. She told me that if I'd gone an hour without throwing up, I was in the clear. It was arbitrary, probably, but years later I thought of that each time I got sick, watched the clock and hoped that once sixty minutes had gone by, I could feel soothed by the idea that it was over, had passed.

I wanted someone to tell me that if I hadn't had a panic attack for three days it meant I was okay, I could relax, that I could reassure myself that everything was going to be fine. As if it were that simple, so black and white. As if my mother's mental illness was or wasn't. Was either all-encompassing or nonexistent. And this was something I would always wonder about—how the lines were drawn to define mental illness. When did a little depression become pathological?

When did anxiety turn into something bigger, something greater and more cautionary about your own stability?

I thought about that picture of my mother and her prom date often, as a little reminder to never stop worrying about the possibility of my own illness, to constantly analyze my own behavior, to continually fear an impending psychotic break, so as to never be caught by surprise. As if my own anxiety could somehow soften the blow.

Earlier in the day I'd gotten a text from Phil. *Hey, hope you're doing well out there. Just wanted to say hi. Saw my brother today, think he'll be coming home soon. And passed by your mom in the hall, she smiled at me.*

What did that mean? I analyzed it from a hundred different angles. A smile seemed so loaded. Had my mother recognized him? Was she happy? Or was she lost, and smiling at a faraway thought in her head? Was it a simple, friendly gesture? But that in itself would've meant so much. I started to fall asleep picturing my mother's smile, the subtle nod of her head as she acknowledged Phil, the brightening of her eyes telegraphing some semblance of normalcy.

THE next afternoon, my grandmother drove me to the airport. We were stopped at a light and I pulled the visor down, trying to block the Florida sun, so bright and unrelenting. My grandmother's nails were painted the color of coral. Her hands were firmly stationed at ten and two; she didn't take her eyes off the road but said clearly, pointedly, "It will take so long for you to understand this, but you can't punish yourself for someone else's pain. You have to learn to separate, to draw boundaries. It's the hardest thing, loving your mother. It's the most profound and heartbreaking, the most important, love of my life. But I also couldn't let it define me. I had another daughter. I had grandchildren. I had my own sense of self. And now I have Saul too."

Earlier that morning I'd been flipping through the pages of *Anna Karenina*, and I came across this sentence toward the end: *But the law of loving others could not be discovered by reason, because it is unreasonable.* There was such a comfort in those words. Yes, it was impossible to control whom I loved and why, and just as my family had no choice but to love my mother, I had not chosen whatever complicated feelings I felt for Daniel or Phil. There was nothing to be done about that. All I could do was try my best to navigate through the tangled mess of loss and longing.

※

I was two hours early for my flight and I sat at the counter of an express California Pizza Kitchen at the airport, eating a miniature BBQ chicken pizza sprinkled with purple slices of onion. I took out my phone and a moment later Daniel called.

"That's so, so weird," I said. "I literally just took out my phone to text you."

"Oh nice. I'm out walking Stella , just wanted to say hi. What time is your flight?"

"It's not until three but I'm already here, actually."

"Do you want me to pick you up from the airport?"

"No, but thanks, that's sweet. I think my dad will get me." That was a lie. My father had a PTA meeting after school that night, but I couldn't allow Daniel to do anything that nice for me. I'd been hoping that he wouldn't be thoughtful or considerate. I had been wanting him to fail me.

"Okay, well maybe we can just hang out after? I'll drive out to your place."

"Perfect," I said. "I should be home by seven or so."

chapter
17

DANIEL and I were at an old-school Italian place decorated with red-and-white checkered vinyl tablecloths and tarnished statues of the Virgin Mary.

"Tell me what you did while I was gone," I said. He looked so cute, in a navy plaid shirt and his rectangular-framed glasses, which he so rarely wore instead of his contacts. I felt a surge of tenderness and then I hated myself for it, for everything. For fucking things up, for wanting more than he could give me.

"Um, let me think," Daniel said. "Kyle and I went to the movies last night, and the day before that I did nothing. The weather has been really shitty. Oh, over the weekend my mom and I went to see these new copper sculptures at MOMA."

Daniel and I didn't care about the same things. This had always been somewhat of an issue for us, but its importance came and went. He loved visual art, had always felt connected to it in a way that I wished I could understand. It was a flaw of mine, I knew, but when he talked about it—complementary colors and the ways that blues and oranges perfected and harmonized each other—when he told me that I didn't look at paintings properly, said I was just looking *at* them, not *into* them, I didn't know what he meant and I tended to just zone out. And that was what happened to him when I talked about books. We tried but were always looking past each other. Once, we got into a big argument at an art museum in Philadelphia where we'd gone on a school trip. There was a slanted line of charcoal against an otherwise empty canvas—I just couldn't see the beauty in it and I accused him of lying when he said he did.

But on this night we were both present and I was trying to be a good girlfriend, to connect even if I wanted to check out while he was telling me about the way the sculptures inhabited the room, something about the images in negative space. I leaned over a wicker basket of bread and took his hand. And then I told him the story about my Grandma Ruth reading *Anna Karenina* to her own grandmother as a child. I told him how comforting it felt to be connected to my family. How I was planning to visit my mother tomorrow. How I felt this rush of optimism. I went on and on.

"I'm sorry I'm talking so much," I said. "I just feel this weight lifted somehow. I needed my grandmother to tell me that things were going to work out, and even though I know she doesn't have any definitive answers, she made me feel better anyway."

"That's great," Daniel said. He scattered a handful of oregano over his slice of pizza. "I'm really glad you went."

※

BACK at my house, Daniel and I lay on my bed, and I showed him some pictures on my phone from Florida. One of Saul and my grandmother that they didn't know I'd taken—they had both been asleep by the pool, lying on plastic beach chairs, their hands dangling toward each other, fingers intertwined.

My phone buzzed and a text from Phil appeared, plainly, on the screen.

I really want you to come home. Is that bad?

I pressed a button and it was gone, but already my stomach was churning. I slid my fingers across the screen, kept showing Daniel pictures, but I knew there was something hurried, frantic, in my gestures.

"Who was that?" he asked. "Who's Phil?"

"Hmm?"

"Emma, who *is* he?"

"No one, he's just this guy, a friend of mine."

"A friend of yours?"

Daniel sat up, and I did the same, folding my legs beneath me.

"Yes . . ."

"That's not really an answer," he said, the pitch of his voice rising. "How did you meet him? How come you haven't told me about him?"

"He's just a friend of Annie's brother. And his brother is in the same hospital as my mom."

"And?"

"And *what?*" I asked.

He looked at me expectantly.

"That text was not nothing. 'Is that bad?' Come on. What the fuck?"

"No Daniel, stop, it's not like that. Seriously."

"Come on! Give me a break, you think I'm an idiot?"

"It's not a thing," I said. "It really isn't." I kept saying it, but I was lying and it was getting worse, my voice growing more desperate. I watched Daniel pick at a flap of skin at the side of his thumb, something he often did when he was agitated or angry.

"What the fuck! You're totally lying. You are totally, totally full of shit. You're sleeping with this guy?"

"I'm not, Daniel! Please, please, just listen to me."

"Then what is it? It's just some platonic thing? You guys just saw each other at the hospital and you really connected and it's so romantic but you really care about me and you don't want to hurt me? Is that it? That is so big of you, thank you so much!"

"I mean, I don't know, Daniel. I guess it's not just totally platonic but it's also not a big deal, it's just . . ."

"Will you please stop saying my fucking name!"

"I'm so, so sorry." I reached to touch his hand so that he would stop tearing at his thumb, which was raw and starting to bleed, but he flinched.

"This is bullshit," he said. "I'm going home." He put his sneakers on, tied the laces of his Pumas, in quick, severe motions.

"Please, please, please don't leave. I'm so sorry. I'm sorry I didn't tell you about him sooner, but it's not a thing, I just didn't want to make a big issue out of it."

"Can you just stop talking!" He stood up and grabbed his sweatshirt, which had been draped over the chair at my desk.

"You're going? You're gonna drive home now?"

"Yup."

"Daniel, come on."

"No, fuck you! You have this holier-than-thou thing about your mom being sick and then you're picking guys up at the hospital?"

"It's so, so, so not like that!"

"Whatever. It doesn't matter," he said, his voice suddenly weary with something like resignation.

"But it does matter!" I said.

He walked out the door, and then briskly through the living room, where my father was sitting in an arm chair, his legs crossed, reading a book. I was directly behind Daniel. My father looked up at me and we exchanged the briefest of glances, but I wasn't going to make a scene in front of him. I felt the heat of embarrassment and shame as I chased Daniel out the door.

"You're seriously just leaving?"

"Yes." He was in the car, his navy Subaru, and his headlights flashed on and cast a bright glow against my neighbor's garage.

"Can you just roll down your windows for a second?"

"What?"

I hurried around the driveway and got into the car with him.

"Please, just let me sit for a minute."

I sat there and I wept, and Daniel was motionless beside me, his hands firmly on the wheel. He stared ahead blankly, with this stony look on his face.

"Daniel, please. You have to forgive me."

"For what?"

But I had nothing to say, could not say it. "I just . . . I just."

"You're pathetic, Emma."

"Please . . ."

"Say it, just say what you fucking did. Say your mother is sick and you used it as an excuse to pretend I'm not a real person, an excuse to go fuck some other guy and ruin everything."

There was something in the way he said "ruin," the indignation in his voice, and I thought of something being violently destroyed, imploding, a building collapsing into itself. Everything was falling apart and he was right, I had ruined it.

"I'll do anything. I'll do everything in the world for you to forgive me."

"You understand that what we had was basically perfect and you ruined it, right?"

I tried to catch my breath, and wiped my face with the side of my sleeve.

"I'm gonna go back to school tomorrow," Daniel said. "Let's just take a little time away from each other, okay?"

I stared at the tiny flecks of green in his eyes. He looked so different at this moment—so wounded, so much more vulnerable than I had allowed him to be these last few weeks.

"Please get out," he said softly. "Please, please just get out of my car."

And I did.

He backed out and was gone, leaving a trail of exhaust, thick and gray, in his wake.

I went back inside, past my father, and then went out the side door of the kitchen into the backyard. The air was icy and still, and I sat down on the grass, which was brittle and damp with frost. This space had once seemed so enormous to me; it was where my mother and I used to pick blueberries, where my old cat Miles was buried, where, briefly, my father had erected a swing set, though it wasn't sturdy enough and collapsed under the weight of a brief storm. But as I sat there now, the yard felt suffocatingly small.

I decided to smoke what was left of the small, stale joint I'd hid in my underwear drawer before I'd left for Florida. I had never smoked by myself before, but at this moment it didn't really seem to matter. I would've done anything to not have to sit with myself, alone with my thoughts. The joint was so tiny and close to my face that when I lit it, I accidentally singed the tips of my eyelashes. Two or three of them fell off and landed on my knee, thin and fractured like broken insect wings. I inhaled. I didn't know if Daniel was right about everything. Was everything good with us before I did this? Had I destroyed the last remaining stable thing in my life? But I took a deep breath and told myself I didn't care. Couldn't care. I wanted to only think about my mother. Fuck everything else. *Fuck it, fuck it, fuck everything*, I thought.

chapter
18

ANNIE was back in town and when I asked if she'd come to the hospital with me she said *yes, of course,* and offered to drive. I didn't tell her about what happened with Daniel or Phil. I couldn't bring myself to utter the words out loud, as if the moment the words left my mouth, they'd become crystallized and somehow even more true.

We were in her mother's car—a long silver Caravan that was probably ten years old. It had a CD player and glove compartment stuffed with vinyl books bulging with discs, old mixes that we made or CDs that Annie loved when she was a kid. I flipped through the pages, shrieking every so often when I came across an album I was particularly nostalgic for. "Is it okay if we talk about stupid stuff?" Annie asked. We were driving west toward Rockland County. It was noon on a Wednesday, and the road was empty ahead of us, the sun a vivid yellow, slanting through the bare branches and onto the evenly paved highway.

"Please," I said. "Of course. All I want to do is talk about stupid stuff."

"I just don't want you to feel like I'm babbling away about these things that are pretty inconsequential when you have real shit going on."

"It's not like that," I said. "I promise. I want to be distracted and not think about all this stuff anyway."

Annie had been in Colorado, skiing with Henry and his family, and apparently they kept bumping into a family friend, Tessa, who Henry had dated every summer at camp until just before sophomore year. She said Tessa just always seemed to be around, and how it seemed so obvious there was still something between the two of them. And later, back at home, Annie had opened up Henry's desk drawer and found a picture of them together after some camp formal. She felt sick to her stomach seeing the way he'd looked at her. They hadn't been together in over a year, but was he *really* over it?

The story continued for a long while and I felt so relieved to be able to talk to Annie this way—to just listen and empathize, to be able to offer even the *slightest* bit of helpful advice.

"Think about the way you feel about Alex," I said, referring to her ninth grade boyfriend, who'd broken her heart. "Maybe there's some nostalgia and Alex will always occupy this specific place in your memory, in your thoughts or whatever, but Henry's the one you *want* to be with."

"You're right," Annie said, "I do."

We put on the *Almost Famous* soundtrack, sang along to "Tiny Dancer," and reenacted the scene where the band is on a small plane and they're caught in an electrical storm and think they're about to die. One by one the characters began to shout out all their secrets.

"I once hit a man in Dearborn, Michigan!" Annie yelled.

"I'm gay!" I cried.

"I slept with Marna!"

"My mom is in a mental hospital!" I yelled, breaking character.

"Oh, Emma," she said, "stop." She lowered the music.

"I just want to warn you," I said, "I don't know what my mother's going to be like in there. I'm just saying, I hope she isn't—"

"Stop," Annie said. "It doesn't matter, whatever she's like, it's fine."

❈

MY mother was meeting with a doctor when we got there, so Annie and I sat down in the dining hall, and picked at a big plastic bowl filled with pretzel Goldfish. There were squares of origami paper littered throughout the room on tabletops. They were in loud, bright colors: pinks and yellows, some gold and shimmery.

"I used to love origami," Annie said.

"You and me both."

But I couldn't remember how to make anything—none of those dainty cranes or butterflies, so I made a fortune teller instead. I folded the paper into one triangle and then another, labeled the sleeves with colors and numbers, wrote my hidden messages beneath them.

I put my fingers into the folds and asked Annie to choose. Her possible futures:

You and Henry will live happily ever after.

You and I will live happily ever after.

You will get five hundred followers on Twitter.

You will get a five on your American History AP test.

You will get a perfect score on your SATs and will get into every college you apply to.

"I love them, I love them all!" Annie squealed. And I thought about how easy it was to view someone else's future in a way that was so optimistic and full of hope. Why did it feel impossible to do the same about my own?

My mother came out a little while later. She looked good—a lot better than the last time I saw her here before I'd left for Florida, but there was still something glazed, a little bit far away, in her eyes. She was wearing a purple cardigan that I'd packed for her when she first got here, which somehow felt like forever ago.

"Mom, I brought Annie with me. I hope that's okay." She didn't say anything but Annie stood up and they embraced each other. Annie towered over her, which she had ever since the summer after eighth grade. I watched as my mother rubbed Annie's back, just once, but it felt like such a sweet, loaded gesture.

The visit passed quickly. We all sat down at the table and spent the next hour folding and twisting the squares of paper, constructing miniature creatures, flowers and trees, a pineapple. My mother surprised me, her deft, gifted fingers moved so quickly, so expertly, and I thought of her playing the piano so beautifully all through the years of my childhood.

※

ANNIE and I spent the next twenty-four hours together. After the hospital we stopped and got Thai food, then went back to her house. Then we got into her bed and watched a marathon of *America's Next Top Model*. We hadn't done this—spent all this time together, alone—in so long. It felt like the most perfect way to spend the night. At some point I got a text from Phil: *Should I not have said that?* I silenced my phone, slid it back into the pocket of my sweatshirt. It wasn't just that I felt guilty about Daniel. I felt embarrassed too that I had handled all of it so badly, and it was just a sign of my immaturity. I imagined Phil saying he didn't want to get involved in my high school drama. I didn't want to tell him what had happened and yet I couldn't bring myself to act normally and just text him back.

※

ANNIE'S mother knocked on the door and simultaneously opened it—this was something my mother always did too, and Annie and I constantly complained about it. *What's the point of knocking if you're just going to open it anyway?* I'd ask.

Annie's mother smiled, maybe beamed, when she saw me.

"Emma!" she said, clearly pleased. "Look at this. Everything's as

it should be—you guys in bed together, some awful TV show on in
the background—it's almost as though you never went to boarding
school!"

＊

ANNIE drove me home the next evening. It was just before six and
the sky was dusky and blue, the sun quietly receding. That lonely
time of day. My father was in the kitchen making dinner and I could
smell the onions and peppers cooking, sizzling with cumin or chili
powder. I went into my bedroom and closed the door. I needed to
lie down—I was feeling so adrift and untethered, dizzy with anxiety.
Maybe it was saying goodbye to Annie, or Daniel having gone, but
suddenly my heart was beating wildly, pounding against my chest, as
if it was trying desperately to get my attention.

It was happening again. I thought in Florida that this phase of
acute anxiety had passed, but it struck me in that moment that
maybe it never really would. I felt a wave of dread and something
like terror as I imagined the next years of my life, constantly punctuated with this kind of panic. How would I ever be happy if I was
always anticipating this feeling, wherever I was, no matter what I
was doing?

I felt nauseous and somehow lost. Where the fuck was I? Was
this what it felt like to lose touch with reality? Was I delusional?
Was I one of those people who heard voices, who was commanded
to do horrible, inexplicable things like drive a station wagon full of

children into a river? What was happening? I wanted to call Daniel's mother, but I couldn't, not anymore.

Some toxic combination of guilt and panic was coursing through my body like an autoimmune disease and I wanted it out. The only way I could think of was through that cigarette lighter, the heat of the flame against my skin. But I wouldn't do it, didn't want any more scars, any more evidence of pain.

My father knocked on the door. I didn't know how to tell him that I needed him without telling him that I needed him.

"Yeah?"

"Dinner's ready," he said. "I made chicken fajitas."

"Okay." My voice was muffled beneath a pillow.

"You all right?"

I didn't answer.

"Can I come in for a second?"

The lights were off in my room, the screen saver on my old desktop computer aglow, a cube of colors against a black sky, morphing into one shape and then another. I'd been feeling so angry at my father and I didn't quite know why, but I was buckling under the weight of it now.

"Dad," I said finally, "I'm freaking out. I'm really freaking out."

Aside from brief hugs that my father and I had given each other when I was coming or going from school, we hadn't really touched in years. There'd always been something stiff about our interactions, some reserved quality between us. (This was always something about

Daniel and his family that I'd been envious of, the way there seemed to be an easiness between them, their affection flowing so freely.) It had been years since I'd allowed myself to be so openly emotional in front of my father, and finally I started to cry, really weep, and collapse into his arms.

"I know it's so hard," he said, "and I'm sorry if sometimes I don't acknowledge how difficult all of this is. It's such a struggle, I know, but we'll be okay. We just will. There isn't any other option."

"I just want everything to go back to normal," I said. "I just want to feel normal."

Everything seemed so off, so skewed, as if I was in some weird version of my own life. As if I was trying to find the right setting on the television, and each button I pressed left the screen a little distorted, a little more out of focus.

When my panic finally abated, my father reheated dinner and we prepared our fajitas together. We spread guacamole over the tortillas, filled them with chicken and peppers and a dash of sour cream.

There was nothing so good as the feeling of calm that settled in the wake of anxiety. If only there were a way to hold onto it, to savor that weightlessness, the pure feeling of relief that was so close to elation.

After dinner we sat in the living room together and read. I'd finally been able to sink into *Anna Karenina*—the torrid affair, Anna's intense longing for Vronsky.

I looked over at my father and asked him what he was reading.

He lifted the book up toward me.

"It's about Robert Moses."

"Wait, remind me who he is again?"

"He was a really influential urban planner in the forties and fifties. He's responsible for so many big changes in New York." My father lifted his glasses up off his face, leaned toward me the way he always did when he started on a subject he felt excited about.

"But he was also grossly racist and his planning was inherently skewed to favor the rich. It's really almost sickening to read about."

"How was it skewed?"

My father told me about the highways that were built with overpasses that were too small to allow buses to go through, so poor people would be restricted to certain areas. He told me about parks and pools built only in wealthy white neighborhoods. For a moment, I felt in awe of him again, his knowledge, his passion.

"And another thing," my father continued, "he was also sort of responsible for the demolition of the old Penn Station, which was an extraordinarily beautiful building. It's a shame you'll never get to see it. You would have loved it."

"That's so sad. The one now is just so ugly."

"I know. Here, hold on."

He got up and walked toward the book shelf at the other end of the room. He scanned the rows and rows of shelves, and then bent down to choose a handful of the larger ones on the bottom, hardcover books of photographs.

"Look, here it is." He opened a coffee-table-sized book of black-and-white pictures, old New York in sepia-toned images. The beautiful Penn Station with its lofty arched ceilings and marble columns. He turned the pages, showed me the elevated train tracks that ran along Third Avenue, and the Williamsburg Bridge being built.

We looked at old photographs together, compared street corners a hundred years apart, cobblestone ripped up and smoothed with cement, tenements torn down, replaced with high-rises. He seemed almost in pain as he showed me all the beautiful old landmarks that had been demolished. My father and I, we were both so fixated on preserving the past.

chapter
19

WHEN we arrived at the hospital on Saturday, my mother was sitting in the day room next to her roommate, Debbie. She was shuffling a deck of UNO cards and Debbie was engrossed in a biography of Axl Rose.

"Debbie loves Guns N' Roses," my mother whispered. There was a slight lilt in her voice, suggesting something like sarcasm, and I reveled in it, this small indication that my mother, the music snob, was coming back to me, coming back to her old self.

I could somehow feel Phil's presence before I saw him—a slight tingling in my stomach, some charge in the air, and there he was. Dressed in washed-out jeans, a bit baggy because he probably hadn't put them in the laundry for weeks, a button-down shirt, and his hair the slightest bit shaggy. It had only been a week since I'd seen him but I registered all the subtle differences I could possibly detect, filling in the spaces of all the things I didn't really know about him.

He lifted a small duffel bag over his shoulder and stood beside his mother. She was tall and slim, with dark hair and a wide streak of silver near her bangs. She was looking intently at someone—a doctor or psychologist, somebody talking kindly, gesturing in a warm but authoritative way. I heard the words *recovery* and *promise, strength.* Ted, Phil's brother, was standing next to them, modestly bowing his head a bit, but he looked a little more poised than he had in the past. His face a little more animated. He smiled and shook the doctor's hand.

Phil and I made eye contact for a moment and then I approached him. Last night I'd finally texted him back and apologized for not being in contact sooner. *Things have been so hectic,* I said. This was obviously an oversimplification. There were too many things going on in my head, and I worried that if we actually spoke, all of my anxiety and guilt and confusion would pour out. I wasn't ready to let him see that part of myself.

"Hey," he said coolly. "Ma, Ted, this is Emma, she's a friend of Zach's sister." I loved the way he said *Ma.* And this small interaction felt so telling, the way he introduced me as Annie's friend and not his own. The way he didn't move forward to greet me, just stood there stiffly. I realized then how little I really knew about him. I had pieced together the small details he'd offered me: his mother from Cuba, his parents working hard and not being able to visit the hospital often. I had created a portrait in my head of a hardworking, stereotypical immigrant family. And on some level, I had used that to keep comparing Phil to Daniel, whose family had so much privilege. But really, I had made it all up. Maybe Phil had a trust fund, maybe his parents worked a lot because they were corporate lawyers. Maybe I didn't know him at all.

His mother nodded and smiled. "Nice to meet you."

"You're heading home?" I asked Ted, though it was obvious that he was.

"I am," he said. "It's been a long time coming."

"That's so great," I said. "My mom's here. I hope she'll be coming home soon too."

They all nodded, and Phil shifted the bag from one shoulder to the other.

"Well, it was nice to see you," he said, "but we should probably take off."

"Of course," I said. "Congratulations on going home, Ted."

I wanted Phil to hang back for just a moment, to let us talk, but he was the first to start walking, his mother and Ted following behind him, and within seconds they were gone.

✳

WE met up the next afternoon, Phil and I. The weather was grim— cloudy and cold, the sky the color of slate. He agreed to pick me up and then we drove around aimlessly for a while. I didn't tell him about what happened with Daniel, how he saw the text message and how maybe it was all over—I wanted to maintain at least a shred of dignity.

"I'm so sorry that I took so long to get back to your texts," I said, even though I had already apologized about this the night before, over the phone. I hated the idea that I'd messed things up between us somehow, even though obviously it was a ridiculous notion. "My life just feels so chaotic right now. And I feel stupid dragging you into this cluttered, shitty situation."

"I didn't mean to complicate things," Phil said. His eyes were focused on the road ahead of him. He switched gears effortlessly.

"You didn't," I said. "It's not like that."

We were stopped at a light and I stared at a pair of pigeons who were walking delicately on a telephone wire, like tiny acrobats on a tightrope. He was silent.

"I really like you," I told him. "Obviously. I just feel like such a mess. I really need to figure some stuff out."

He moved his hand into my lap, and I took it eagerly, held onto his fingers with both hands. I was feeling overwhelmed with tenderness and desire, but then I stopped myself. I thought about Daniel. I thought of my mother and I focused on those images of her sitting idling at the supermarket on that frigid night.

"You want me to take you to make-out point? Where I take all the girls?"

I felt a twinge of jealousy as he said this. I knew he was joking but I also knew instinctively that there had been so many girls.

"Absolutely," I said. "But I'm not making out with you."

He laughed. "Fair enough."

We drove a little while longer, down Route 35 and then onto a small gravel road. There was an empty white hatchback parked diagonally along the path, and we pulled over nearby. We faced an expanse of water, silver and still.

"The reservoir," he said. We got out of the car and walked toward it, sat down on a ledge of rocks. "This is where we used to go in high school, have bonfires and smoke weed and drink forties and think we were so cool."

"Ah, the cool kids."

"I had sex in that water after prom," he whispered.

"You were such a bad boy."

I imagined his high school love, whoever she was, beautiful and self-possessed, a "free spirit" who would spontaneously shed all her clothes and dive into the water. That first day when Phil and I drove up to the hospital together, on New Year's Eve, we were listening to some classic rock station and "Norwegian Wood" had come on, and he'd told me this was the song he always thought of when he thought of his ex-girlfriend. *I once had a girl, or should I say, she once had me.* I wondered if this was the girl he was talking about, the one he had been so taken with.

"I'm thinking of not going back to school this semester," he said unexpectedly.

"Are you serious?"

"Yeah, I know, it sounds stupid. It just feels too hard to go back right now. Maybe I can just make up the classes over the summer or something."

"But you're at Purchase, it's so close," I said. "Can't you just come home and visit a lot? Like, on the weekends and stuff. I mean you could probably even live at home if you wanted."

"Yeah I know," he said, sounding the slightest bit impatient. "Anyway it's not a big deal, I just need to think about it."

I started to wonder if maybe I shouldn't go back to school either, if it was possible for me to transfer back to public school here for second semester. The thought hadn't really occurred to me to stay in Westchester. Or maybe it had, but I hadn't seriously considered it. The fact was, while I felt a sharp sting of dread when I thought about returning to school, I didn't really want to stay here either. I wanted to get swept up in the everyday activities of classes and library and homework, watching TV in the common room with my roommates, smoking cigarettes and masking the smell by exhaling onto sheets of fabric softener. I wanted some semblance of what passed for a normal life.

※

LATER, on the drive home, I asked Phil what it was like having his brother back home.

"It's good and bad," he answered. "I'm so glad he's back, but it's also going to be a big adjustment for him. A transition, you know. So it's going to take some time. He's a little shell-shocked, I think."

"But how is it for *you*?"

He laughed. "You sound like my therapist."

"But really, I'm asking."

"It's gonna take time for me too, I guess. I'm a little bit walking on eggshells. I just keep wondering how long it'll be until we'll be able to get into a fight. Until I'll be able to take the remote from him and say that I *need* to watch the hockey game. Until I'll be able to be in a bad mood in front of him, you know what I mean? All that stuff."

"I haven't even thought about that at all," I said. "Like, when can I be a brat and snap at my mom if she wakes me up too early and I'm cranky?"

"Exactly."

"That feels like such a luxury."

"One day!" Phil said dreamily. "One day you'll be able to be a little bitch to your mom and it'll be all okay again."

I laughed. "Shut up! I'm not a *bitch* per se, but you know what I mean."

"Of course, but seriously, like the goal is to be able to just be normal, and maybe that means being an asshole every so often and having that be okay."

We were back at my house then, where my father's Volvo rested in the driveway and I could see the dim yellow light in my parents' bedroom. I watched my father's silhouette move around, open up a dresser drawer.

"I'm leaving for school in two days," I told Phil. "But maybe we can talk and I'll let you know when I'm back here?"

"Of course."

I kissed his face, his cheekbones, the soft skin beside his ear. I was careful not to touch his lips, as if any of those arbitrary rules really mattered, as if we hadn't already had sex and I hadn't probably ruined my relationship with Daniel.

"I know this sounds so completely sentimental," I warned, "but

I just feel so happy that we met, despite how fucked up the circumstances were."

"You mean so happy that you were my tattoo artist, that fateful night?"

"Yes, exactly," I said. "That fateful night."

＊

I already felt a pang of longing when I got out of the car. I wondered when I would see him again. Wondered if next time, that connection between us—one that felt both so erotic and cerebral—would still be there. Everything felt so impossible to predict, I just didn't know what I would be able to hold on to and what would disappear.

＊

I slipped inside the house and found my father standing in the bathroom, in front of the mirror. His beard was covered in shaving cream and there was an old-school red-and-blue-striped can of Noxzema sitting on the counter.

I asked him if he thought I should stay home and not go back to school next week.

"Absolutely not. No, Emma, you have to go back."

"Okay well I was just asking your opinion, I don't *have to go back*."

"I've already paid for the semester, so in that sense, you do."

"Dad."

He tapped his razor against the inside of the sink.

"I'm sorry," he said. "The real issue is that you should go back

to school for you. You need to carry on with your life. Go to classes. Be with your friends. Do your work. What would you do here
anyway?"

"Visit Mom? Take care of her when she's home?"

"No. And as soon as she gets home, she'll probably go straight into
outpatient treatment anyway."

He dipped his hands into the cloudy water, wiped the rest of the
cream off his face. He looked at me through the mirror.

"We'll figure out a way for you to come back often, okay? I promise."

＊

THE last time I visited my mother before I returned to school, I got
to the hospital just after lunch. I went into the dining room first,
where plastic trays were stacked with empty Jell-O containers and
what looked like the remnants of some sort of fancy, breaded mac
and cheese. My mother wasn't there, and then I found her in the day
room gazing at the large-screen TV. *The Ellen Degeneres Show* was
on, and she was doing some little dance on the stage, her audience
laughing wildly.

"Hi, Mom."

"Oh hi, sweetie." It was the first time that she had addressed me
like this since she'd been in the hospital, and I couldn't help feeling
grateful.

"How are you?" I asked. "What have you been doing today?"

"I'm all right, I met with a therapist for a while, then I played a lot
of Scrabble with Debbie."

"Is she good competition?"

"No, actually she's awful! She kept putting down words that I knew were not in the dictionary, but I didn't have the heart to tell her. She got a triple word score for 'alot.' Like 'a lot' but one word. I tried but couldn't bring myself to tell her."

"Oh, Mom, that's sweet of you."

❄

SINCE my mother had been doing better, the social worker said we could take a walk through the hospital grounds. Outside it was chilly, but warmer than usual; it was too early for spring, but felt as though it was on its way.

We walked through a big open quad, and I imagined it was beautiful and leafy at another time of year. The grass was slightly crunchy beneath our feet; bare trees lined the walkways, their trunks thick and coarse. Add a few Hacky Sacks and students walking hurriedly to class, it could've been any small college across the country. It felt impossible to imagine that I'd be back at school in just a couple of days, swept up into an old and familiar life, a life that right then felt so foreign.

When my mother brought me to Oak Hill that first year, we took a walk around campus as my father finished unloading the car. I'd felt this twinge of homesickness before she even started to say goodbye. I wanted so badly to halt the inevitable progress of my life, the change that had been kicked into motion and couldn't be stopped. Two nights earlier, just before I'd left for Oak Hill, I'd gotten stoned with my friend Josh in his Toyota, and we drove around Scarsdale, exhaling into the warm, balmy air. He kept saying how excited he was for college, how ready he was for his life to start moving forward, and how he envisioned himself on a conveyor belt at the supermarket, like a bag of grapes or a quarter-pound of turkey, sitting on the rubber mat, ready to move, to be carried forward. I thought about this now, how if Josh was sitting idly, ready to go, I was holding on to that metal divider that separates your supermarket purchases, trying desperately not to move ahead. But I also knew that on some level, I had no choice but to submit to this uneasy place where we were, my mother and I, to allow ourselves to be carried along together, to wherever we were going.

MOST of the snow was gone, but there were still patches of ice along the cement path we walked down, and I held on to my mother to steady myself, put my arm through hers. I told her about Daniel, eliminating many of the sorry details, only letting her know that things were shitty—that I'd messed up and felt conflicted about what I wanted from him. She didn't talk much, but she said she thought I needed to be patient, with myself and also with everyone around me. I knew that she was right, but everything at the moment felt so urgent, so in need of immediate attention, that it was hard to be calm and forbearing.

As we turned back toward her building, she told me about the music therapy group she started attending, how much she liked it, and how sometimes it was just so hard for her to articulate things verbally. And how much easier it felt to express herself through music. It was the first time she'd felt any sense of community at the hospital, but there was a collective sense of hope, she said, as she and her fellow patients played on their instruments together, conjuring up a lovely, if tentative, optimism.

"I'm happy for you, Mom," I told her, and I could see her fingers dancing nimbly across the piano keys, giving herself over to her music again, for the first time in a long while.

Some of my own anxieties started to recede as my mother began to get well, but there was still a seed of panic, somewhere inside me, that was always ready to unfurl. We stood outside of her building, and I looked around at this lovely and leafy hospital campus, wondering if it was something like my birthright.

I decided to take the Amtrak back to school because flying felt too fast. I needed the extra time to mentally prepare myself for the change, and I wanted to prolong it as much as I could. The train would be eight hours and would take a non-direct route, north through upstate New York, then west through Syracuse, tracing the border of the state, and then back down through Pennsylvania.

My father drove me to the train station at Croton-Harmon, a town along the Hudson. We got to the station only a few minutes before the train was scheduled to leave and so our goodbye was rushed. But it seemed almost better that way. He told me he loved me, that he'd keep me posted about everything. Assured me that it would all be okay, as if there was any way he could possibly know. But I appreciated his optimism, his need to comfort me.

"Please call me when you get in tonight," he asked.

"It'll be so late, I won't get back to school until after midnight."

"I don't care, just call me. Please," my father insisted.

"Fine," I said. "I love you." And I hurried onto the train, struggling with the weight of my duffel bag as I walked through the aisle, bracing myself on the worn red leather of the seats.

The car must have filled up at Penn Station, and so when I finally found a seat, I was sitting backward, the train thrusting me in one direction, though I was firmly planted in another. The scenery was alternatingly dull and beautiful, with pockets of land that seemed untouched, blanketed in snow.

I looked at my phone. I had called Daniel three times since he left my house that night. He hadn't picked up any of the times. I didn't know what I wanted from him. I didn't know why I was calling. But I couldn't imagine being back at school without him, was terrified by the thought of it.

I opened up *Anna Karenina* again. I had reached the place where, a few weeks ago, I'd written in the car, *this day*. I had wanted so badly, had hoped so ardently, that by the time I reached this chapter in the book, I'd have some better, clearer sense of things. I still didn't know what had changed and what hadn't. I still wanted to know, desperately, what would happen to me. To my mother. And so I moved forward two hundred pages and wrote it again, *this day*.

Maybe Daniel and I would be completely, permanently broken up, maybe I would walk past him in the dining hall, and he would stare down at his tray, careful not to offer me even a flicker of recognition. Or perhaps we would've worked things out, somehow moved beyond everything that had happened. And then there was Phil—would I look back and think that was all some foolish, misguided expression of my grief?

My mother was still in the hospital the day I left for school, but maybe, by the time I was four hundred pages through, she'd be home again. Maybe the next time I saw her, she'd open up the front door of our house, take me in her arms, her fingers aching from the trio of piano lessons she'd given one after the other. Or would she still be at the hospital, feeling aimless, tired, trapped in the complicated mazes of her mind?

There were so many things that I would continue to wonder about. Would this fear of mental illness always plague me and our family? Was there any way to steel myself against it? And mostly, would my mother ever, truly, be well?

But that day on the train, I stretched out onto the empty seat next to me and shut my eyes. What I saw was that image of myself as a child, my small feet perched on the edge of the stepladder in my grandmother's home, staring out the window ahead, looking for my mother, waiting for her to come back to me.

ACKNOWLEDGMENTS

I am so grateful for Michele Rubin's effusive support and motivation during the first part of this process. I definitely would not have had the courage to write this novel without you. To my wonderful agent, Mel Flashman, thank you for your warmth, superb advocacy, and enthusiasm. To Sarah Bush and everyone else at Trident Media, thank you! Rebecca Kilman, my incredible editor, thank you for your brilliant insights and your affection for this project. It has been such a pleasure to work with you. To Marissa Grossman, thank you for coming in at the eleventh hour with so much warmth, energy and dedication. Huge thanks to Ben Schrank, Casey McIntyre, Lauren Donovan, and the rest of the Razorbill/Penguin team.

Thanks also to Rhona Kaplan. To Dan Chaon and everyone else in the amazing Oberlin creative writing community. Thanks to Eli Rosenfeld and Sir Isaac Knewton. Nikki Terry/Orange Custard Design, I am so happy we were able to work together on this project; thank you for your support and kindness and the beautiful website.

To my friends—I am endlessly grateful for all of you, all the time. Special, special thanks to those who have been so loving and supportive throughout this process—you guys are really the best. It should also be noted that one friend encouraged me to write this book in a single Gchat conversation—thanks for that! Seriously: no one, not even the rain, has such good friends.

Lastly, I feel so lucky to come from a family of such wonderful readers and writers. Thank you to my CBC. To Sara Mark and Ellen Umansky, thank you so much for your love, support, and enthusiasm for all things family and literary. To my best bro, Sam Axelrod, for being the most thoughtful and critical reader and also the best at tidying up the house. Your book is next. To my father, George Axelrod, thank you for always encouraging and nurturing my creativity (beginning with tri-Elvis). To my mother, Marian Thurm, my most trusted reader and editor, thank you for everything. I feel so lucky to have inherited a fraction of your gift. And thanks to all my Thurm-related family (Coop included) for everything, always. I love you.